LUNA STATION
QUARTERLY

Issue 035 | September 2018

Editor-in-Chief
Jennifer Lyn Parsons

Editors
Linda Codega • Wanda Evans • Caroljean Gavin
Shel Graves • Cathrin Hagey • Michele Howe • Dana Mele
Kimbery Rei • Kimberly Osgood • Danielle Perry • Gô Shoemake

LUNA STATION PRESS
NEW JERSEY

First Paperback Edition September 2018
ISBN: 978-1-949077-00-1

Luna Station Quarterly publishes short fiction on March 1st, June 1st,
September 1st, and December 1st. For more information and submission
guidelines, please visit our website at lunastationquarterly.com

LUNA STATION PRESS

For Luna Station Press

Creative Director - Tara Quinn Lindsey
Editor-in-Chief & Founder - Jennifer Lyn Parsons

www.lunastationpress.com

CONTENTS

EDITORIAL...6
Jennifer Lyn Parsons

ONE LAST RIDE ON THE HORSE
WITH PURPLE ROSES..12
Jennifer Lee Rossman

TO WALK FOR THE FIRST TIME..20
Erin K. Wagner

WINTER FLOWERS...32
Alessia Galatini

THE MOTHERSHIP...44
K. Bannerman

SPACE WITCH...54
Richaundra Thursday

NECROMANCE...60
Alyssa Striplin

DRAGON FRUIT...68
Izzy Varju

PULLING SECRETS FROM STONES...................................78
Beth Goder

CHECKMATE...94
J.S. Veter

A DREAM OF THIS LIFE...104
Andrea Blythe

THE GHOL.. 116
Rose Strickman

FAITHFUL... 132
Patricia Correll

PHALIUM ARIUM SSP. ANAMS 138
Victoria Sandbrook

RAIN LIKE DIAMONDS 144
Wendy Nikel

BETTER YOU THAN ME... 150
Natalia Yanchak

ESCAPE... 160
K.G. Anderson

THANK YOU TO OUR SUPPORTERS............................ 185
ABOUT THE COVER ARTIST 187

Editorial

Jennifer Lyn Parsons

A software engineer by trade, Jennifer is a life-long lover of story with a capital S. Her work has been seen in various magazines and she has published three books, with quite a few more in her back pocket. She counts Jim Jarmusch and Laura Ingalls Wilder as two of her biggest influences. Make of that what you will.

When not writing either code or fiction, she reads books and comics, and sometimes makes things out of wool or paper. She finds joy in making things, be they digital or analog.

For the last year or so I've written a lot about using stories as self care, a balm for the soul in dark times. This remains a way of using stories that rings true for me, but for the last month or so I have also started turning to stories for something else: a guide on grit and determination.

I was not wrong to seek a balm at first. Things were growing darker and trying to make sense of all the change and raising a fist against the downward slide is exhausting. Stories provided a safe haven from the storm.

As the last couple of years have slid by, I now find that what I envisioned as blackest night to be but a pale shade of grey in comparison to the void before us. Soothing the soul is not enough anymore. Somehow we need to rise each morning with the energy to live our daily lives, as well as fighting the good fight.

We still need to write, create, work, tend the garden, clean the bathroom, etc. etc. If we're caught in a cycle of news, burnout, and righteous anger, the daily work starts to lose significance and fall to the wayside. As our Creative Director, Tara Lindsey likes to say: We need to be present in our lives and make sure we live a good life each day, whatever that means to you.

A valid outlook, but I'm left wondering how to be more present without missing what's going on. More importantly, I wonder how to balance that without burning the candle at both ends and being overwhelmed by it all.

Grit and determination become tools we use to keep our precious lives in repair for the return of the light. Though I honestly wonder now if that day will ever come. If it does not, then developing that grit is even more important than ever.

Where do we look for guides on how to work while in the darkness and keep our faces turned to the light? Stories are always there for us. Their characters show us how to face down the challenges before us, push beyond what we think we can do, and triumph.

My personal favorite is Aerin from "The Hero and the Crown" by Robin McKinley, who was never a favorite, an unwanted, untrusted girl who, defying her role and everyone's desire that she hide herself, rode off to face the deadly Maur. Overcoming what happened to her in the aftermath required nothing short of a spectacular force of will (and an amazing horse).

But it is not just to the obvious warrior we can look for this kind of strength. Many characters wield a softer strength that is long lasting as well.

An old favorite Molly Grue comes to mind, from "The Last Unicorn". She knows beauty and innocence and magic when she sees it and despite being none of these things, by her own admission, still she defends it with all of the tools at her disposal.

There are so many others of course. Meg from "A Wrinkle in Time", Hermione Granger, Princess Leia, pretty much any character Tamora Pierce has ever written.

You may note a pattern here. All of these characters live in a particular type of book, and I don't mean fantasy. They're all now considered Young Adult (thereabouts) and that says something about what we've felt, for decades, is important for young people to learn:

The challenges we face are hard, they will wear you down, they will leech darkness into the world if we let them. Yet, we must engage with them, our friends alongside us whenever possible, and when we keep our hearts open and full of love, they can be overcome.

These challenges are in the micro and the macro, the world events and the daily grind. I'm right here beside you, holding my own head up as best I can. The stories in these pages are full of characters facing their own struggles, some of it world changing, some of it just getting through the day. As you read them, see what you can learn from their successes and failures. See if you can find a way to your own inner grit and determination.

L S Q | 035

One Last Ride on the Horse with Purple Roses

Jennifer Lee Rossman

Jennifer Lee Rossman is an incurable science fiction geek. Her work has been featured in several anthologies and her time travel novella Anachronism is now available from Kristell Ink, an imprint of Grimbold Books. She blogs at jenniferleerossman.blogspot.com and tweets @JenLRossman

Eleanor held the little monster's paw as they walked through the park, ignoring the stares and laughter from passersby. This was their day, their *last* day, and she would not let anyone ruin it.

The world did not exist. Not politics, the economy, nor the latest scandal in the entertainment industry. None of it. The entire universe had been shrunk to a tiny, bright bubble around the two of them, and nothing could break its surface.

"Shall we get ice cream?" Eleanor asked.

Gidget nodded emphatically. "Yes, please!"

It was still strange to speak to the green monster directly, rather than having Anne relaying the conversation. He was so much fuzzier than Eleanor had ever imagined.

They walked along cobblestone paths that wound through lush gardens, some carefully tended with statuary and elaborate topiaries, and others where miscellaneous wildflowers had been allowed to grow where they pleased. Ducks and toy boats floated on the pond's glassy surface, and from somewhere far in the distance came the brassy calliope music of the carousel.

"What flavor?" Eleanor asked as they approached the ice cream cart.

Gidget thought for a moment, his fanged mouth twisting this way and that. "Strawberry," he growled finally.

"All right—"

"And chocolate. And rocky road. And I want butterscotch syrup and extra rainbow sprinkles."

Eleanor gave him a look. Perhaps Gidget's famous appetite hadn't been Anne angling for a second dessert after all. "Well, I am going to have mint chocolate chip."

"Ooh. Me too," Gidget said. "With rainbow sprinkles."

"Deal." Eleanor smiled at the ice cream man. "Two mint chocolate chips, please. One with rainbow sprinkles."

He raised his eyebrow in amusement, and his gaze traveled down her arm to the hand that held Gidget's paw. A sad recognition came over his face, and he refused her money with a pitying smile.

"I remember you and your little girl," he said as he offered her the two cones.

Eleanor's hesitation must have looked to an outsider like she didn't want to accept his charity, but it was the prospect of having to let go of Gidget's paw that gave her pause. But let go she did, and she and Gidget went to sit on a bench in the shade of a sprawling, ancient oak. Eleanor had to hold Gidget's cone for him, and all his enthusiastic licking didn't seem to make a dent in the green treat, but they both pretended not to notice.

"Can we ride the carousel after this?" Gidget asked in his grumbly little voice, licking ice cream from his nose.

A jolt of panic went through Eleanor's chest. The carousel was so close to the exit, it always marked the end of the day at the park. She couldn't bear for this day to end.

"Maybe later," she said, letting a chip melt in her mouth, trying to wring another precious few seconds from her ice cream cone. "Let's finish eating and then walk around a bit more."

Gidget nodded his agreement.

The carousel music seemed to grow a little louder.

***

Eleanor and Gidget were almost to the front of the line before Eleanor remembered that an invisible monster couldn't get his face painted. And what a sight she must have been, a middle-aged woman talking to herself and holding nobody's hand. What would people say if they saw?

Nothing they weren't already saying. Whispered pity, criticizing gossip about her mental state. As if any of them would fare better if *they* lost a child.

The tinkling big band music seemed closer than ever, as if they might see the bobbing carousel horses peering ominously around any tree, their painted roses and ribbons sparkling in the late afternoon sun.

To hell with what people would say. If this was the last day she would ever spend with some remnant of her daughter, Eleanor wasn't about to let sad smiles and gossip stop her from savoring it.

She looked at the sandwich board of designs the artist had propped up beside her wheelchair. "I'll take a butterfly," Eleanor said, sitting primly on the adjacent stool.

The face painter glanced around for a child before realizing Eleanor was alone.

"Yes, it's for me," Eleanor said as Gidget climbed up into her lap. "And then he would like to be a tiger."

Gidget raised his claws. "Grr."

"Okay," the artist said unsurely, dipping her brush into one of the many pools of paint laid out on her palette. With graceful movements she applied cool strokes of color to Eleanor's face, painting swirling purple wings and pink curlicue antennae. Then she looked to Eleanor's lap, where her hands were positioned as if holding an invisible child.

"A tiger, please," Eleanor reminded gently.

"With big stripes," Gidget added, though of course only Eleanor heard him.

With a humoring smile, the artist loaded her brush with paint and leaned forward, making careful brushstrokes in the air. Gidget's green fur turned orange, and though she hadn't run out of paint, the artist washed her brush in her cup of muddy water anyway and used a fresh one to add bold stripes and dainty whiskers to the monster's face.

"Is... that good?"

Gidget nodded and gave a thumbs-up.

"Splendid," Eleanor translated as Gidget scrambled down from her lap and ran off. "Wait for me!" she cried out, all but throwing money at the patient artist as she hurried after the monster.

"I want to play on the swings," Gidget said, pointing across a field to the shiny playground equipment.

"Not without me." She knew it was irrational, that fear that he might disappear if she lost sight of him. She'd kept a careful watch on Anne all through the treatments, and in the end she'd still lost her.

But she knew Gidget couldn't stay forever. What if he just slipped away while she wasn't looking, and she didn't get to say goodbye?

Gidget waited, pleading for permission to go. When she gave a tiny nod, he was off, running on his fuzzy little legs all the way to the swingsets.

"Stay where I can see you!" Eleanor called out, as if that would make any difference.

Still, the carousel grew louder.

***

They flew a kite, they fed the ducks, they picked pansies and tucked them behind their ears. All of Anne's favorite things.

Anything to stall, to keep the day going just a little longer.

But the sun was low in the orange sky and the music surrounded them, coming from every direction at once and so loud that Eleanor could hardly hear herself think.

She tried to avoid it, tried to go anywhere else in the park. But then they turned a corner, and there it was.

The carousel spun, its mirrors and filigree catching the last gasps of sunlight and casting everything in a warm glow as its sculpted horses danced to the calliope.

Eleanor's breath caught in her throat. No, no, it was too soon, but

Gidget held her hand and led her to the ride and she realized that maybe it was time.

Eleanor stooped to Gidget's level and hugged him tight. It was the last hug she would ever give him, so it had to be a good one. Then she stood back with all the other parents as the carousel slowed to a stop and let another group of children board.

For one terrible second, she lost sight of Gidget among all the children, but then he popped up, seated on a white horse.

Anne's horse.

The one with the cream mane frozen in place as if in a strong wind, and its front hoof raised in an elegant prance. The one with purple roses on its bridle and saddle.

The carousel began to turn, and a tear slid down Eleanor's face.

"Which one's yours?" asked another mother.

Eleanor held her breath as the horse with the purple roses took Gidget out of sight, but he was still there when it came back around, waving his paw and grinning a big, fangy grin.

"Mine?" Eleanor knew enough not to point to the horse with the imaginary rider. "Mine was a little girl named Anne."

This was the first time Eleanor had said her name aloud, the first time she'd used the past tense. It didn't hurt as much as she thought it would.

"We used to come here," she said. "Every Saturday. She loved mint chocolate chip, and getting her face painted like a tiger. Playing on the swings. She loved the carousel most of all."

The horses went around again, and Gidget wiggled in his seat in time to the music.

"Then she got sick. I told myself I could keep her safe if I kept her at home and never let her out of my sight. I still lost her. She..." The word seemed to stick in Eleanor's mouth, like it didn't want to be spoken. "She died anyway, and she never got to ride the carousel again."

She lost sight of Gidget again, and squeezed her hands into fists. Not yet, *not yet*. But there he was, coming around the other side.

"I miss her every day, but Saturdays most of all. So today I did something silly. I took Anne's imaginary friend to the park, because I think he must miss her as much as I do."

The carousel began to wind down, the horses hardly bobbing. Gidget kept waving, but somehow it was different. Somehow, this was goodbye.

Eleanor waved back. "Goodbye, Gidget," she whispered. "If you see Anne, tell her I love her."

The horse with the purple roses came around again, this time without a rider. Eleanor took a deep breath to steady herself, then turned and walked away, letting the sound of the carousel fade into silence.

To Walk for the First Time

Erin K. Wagner

Erin K. Wagner is an assistant professor in the SUNY system. She lives in the Catskills, inspired by Rip Van Winkle's game of nine-pins. Her short speculative fiction has appeared in a number of publications, and her novella is forthcoming with Aqueduct Press.

I was very old when I first learned to walk.

In the long quiet years since my birth, my legs have atrophied. They have grown thin and warped, the dark skin overrun with purple veins. I have lain in a bed all that time, legs stretched out before me on white cotton sheets.

"I miss the silence," I tell my nurse. The breeze that blew the gauzy curtains from the window to my bed. The glimpse of the cool green gardens. The sound of the rain trickling and dripping through the foliage. I miss these too.

My nurse is not allowed to speak to me, but sometimes I imagine that she wants to. I shuffle under her guidance, back and forth, back and forth, across the glossy parquet floor. I grow accustomed to her tight grip on my elbow. My legs hurt, but they grow stronger.

"I miss the stillness," I tell my chancellor. The smell of the lavender tucked between my pillows. The faint music from the phonograph in the corner. The spider-webs trembling in the nooks of the cornices. I miss these too.

My chancellor does not want to speak to me, but sometimes he answers my questions. After all, what good is a chancellor who has no advice?

"The crown prince will be able to ascend to the throne in three months' time. Your regency will be a short one." He does not say, *thanks to the gods*. He did not say *blessedly*. But I hear these words anyways.

"So my brother is dead?" I ask him the first time he explains this. "And his queen? Together? Both at once?"

The chancellor lowers his chin and clears his throat. His skin is white around his lips and nose. "Both at once," he says.

I look down at my feet, bare on the tiled floor. My toes seem small and shriveled, and I marvel at their strength. I am standing on my own.

"And I may leave my room?"

"You must."

I pause a second, studying his face. I test myself, swaying back and forth slightly, feeling the muscles at my heels, my calves, my thighs.

"Show me then," I say. "Show me the palace."

***

"You are lucky to be first-born," I tell my nephew when I first meet him. I try to find some similarity between us, but if there is any, I cannot see it. He is slight and delicate, his fingers like twigs on the harpsichord keys. He continues to play as we talk, and he will not look at me, as if he is afraid to see me. I do not like the music, strident and jangling, but I sway a bit to it anyways. When my body moves, I can feel every part of it, hips and breasts and shoulders. My body feels new and stiff, like clothes too heavily starched.

"Why?" he asks, his voice almost lost between the scales he is practicing.

"Because you were not preserved like me." The notes falter. The boy finally swivels on his seat. He looks up, glancing at my chin, not my eyes.

"What is it like?" He speaks very low, almost whispering. "What is it like to be preserved?"

I place both hands heavily on his shoulders. He feels fragile, thin and breakable. He is tense. He wants to break away. I won't let him squirm.

"You never move," I tell him. "You never talk. You never eat. You are never sick. But you grow old. And no matter how strong the spell, your body begins to fall apart."

My nephew's face crinkles, and he squeezes his eyes shut. He begins to cry. I drop my hands, and he slips off the seat. He runs for the door.

I could have been kinder, I think, taking the boy's place at the instrument. I strike one key, and listen to the note resonate until the sound has entirely died away. I strike another. The wood of the harpsichord has been polished to such a degree that I can see my face in it. I am old and I do not know what I should look like, so I sit for a long time staring at my reflection until even the memory of the music fades. There is only an impression, a foggy idea of me there—white wiry hair and wrinkles, so many wrinkles. I wonder that I cannot feel it more, the sagging skin. But it is all new to me.

***

"Only two months more," the chancellor says to me at breakfast. I stare down at the runny yellow yolks of my eggs. I am surprised. Time moves so quickly. I use my toast to sop up the egg. The chancellor smiles in a suffering sort of way, tolerating my eating habits.

"How did my brother die?" I finally ask the question, mostly because I want to see the smile slide off the chancellor's face.

I imagine I should have asked the question earlier, but I do not care about proprieties. There have been more physical curiosities at hand.

"A disease, a sickness the doctors had never seen. It worked rapidly. We hardly had time to prepare, hardly time to pack the prince off to safety."

The yolk tastes like fat, meat and not meat. It is slippery, slick down my throat. The chancellor looks at me, hearty and hale, making slurping noises as I eat. He is upset. He has been upset for weeks. You can see it in the slope of his shoulders and the jowls of his cheeks. I am almost sorry for him, but it has been hard for me to focus on others.

"How long has he been dead?"

I have never seen my brother, so cannot imagine him a corpse. I cannot imagine him a person.

The chancellor pales. He looks down at his watch, as if it might count the days for him. "Twelve days."

I put the fork down and wipe the crumbs of toast on the

tablecloth. It is very quiet. The room smells suddenly stale and I feel almost sick. Eating is, after all, still new to me.

"So for five days, there was no designated regent. There was no monarch." This is what I say, but it is not what I want to say. I think of what I could have done in five days.

"We worked as quickly as we could," the chancellor says. But I know this is not what he wants to say. And I know what he says is not true.

***

I realize that I must spend my time in a more deliberate manner. A month ago the world was new, but now it already grows pale and old, a moon waning fast in the sky. My knees creak and pop as I walk leaning on my cane, and my hair pulls loose when I comb it in the morning. The flowers from my brother's memorial rot in the hallways as if the maids are too afraid to remove this last testament to the old king. I smell the flowers wherever I go. I think the scent has sunk into my skin, and I am afraid that I am decaying. So I touch my arm, my leg, my belly with trembling fingers and assure myself that I am still there, that I am still whole.

"Let us bring you tea. Sit and rest," the servants say to me, scurrying close behind me, careful not to outpace me.

"I don't want tea," I tell them. "Bring me some alcohol."

They bring it to me with reluctant, disapproving glances. The alcohol burns in my throat, sharp and sour. When I drink it, I feel it hot in my chest, and the heat spurs me on. I quicken my stride.

Until they need you. This is what I should have told my nephew. *You never move. You never talk. You never eat. You are never sick.*

Until they need you. Then they pull you from the womb of your quiet room, your soft music, your dripping leaves. They usher you towards death with a rough hand at the back.

"Bring me the witch," I order my chancellor when he comes up simpering, feigning obeisance. "Bring me the witch who cast the preservation spell."

The chancellor smiles ever so slightly. "She is surely dead." He does not use any honorifics with me. "She was old when you were a baby."

"Search anyway," I tell him. "The old have a way of sticking around."

***

I think it will be too late. Another month has passed. I abandon my cane, even if I am unsteady without it. I use my hand against the wall instead. I feel the texture of the fine-grained wood, the ridged wallpaper, the closely-woven tapestries. I feel the house living and growing beneath my fingers, old but still strong.

I glimpse the preparations for my nephew's coronation. He looks very small, almost consumptive, in the fur-trimmed cloak and the ornate crown. His arms and legs are skinny and knobby. He catches me watching him once. At first, he looks frightened, and he almost turns to ask for help or protection. And then he freezes and something almost like pity flits through his large dark eyes. It makes me angry. I lower my hand from the wall. I stand on my own two feet and feel the whole trembling length of my legs, weaker than his. I scowl at him.

"Madam," a voice breaks my concentration and my anger. The servants have adopted the chancellor's informality. "The witch has come. She is in the drawing room if you wish to receive her."

"They found her?" I realize how much I had expected to be disappointed.

"Finally, yes."

I nod. I turn away from the throne room and my nephew. "Tell her I am coming." The servant races ahead to do as I have asked. There is a pain in my hip as I turn and hobble after her.

I pay very close attention to each detail of the hall and floor, of the wall and ceiling. Tiles and chandelier. I am afraid. Afraid that I will not see them much longer if this witch cannot help me. Though it is not really that I will miss them. After all, I did not miss my old room for long.

***

She sits, small and slight, shriveled and shrunken, on the end of a settee. The fabric of her clothes is heavy and woolen, blending in with the fabric of the cushions beneath her. It works as a sort of camouflage, distracting the eye from her sharp face and sharper eye.

"Do you remember me?" I ask, without pretense or introductory small talk.

She tilts her chin to one side, looks me up and down. Thick, gray, matted hair falls on her shoulder. She doesn't blink. "It's all I am. Memories. And I remember you. Though you were redder-cheeked, fresher-skinned." The way she said *skinned* puts me in mind of the animals strung up on the wall of the huntsman's shed.

I ease myself into a chair opposite her, but close. There is only a spindly-legged table between us. One of the servants has laid out a tea-service. I can smell the strong leaves brewing in the water. "How old are you?"

She does not answer with the labored deflections of a courtier, protesting the question.

"Older than you, younger than some."

I cannot imagine anyone older than her. But perhaps that is what my nephew thinks when he looks at me.

"You cast a preservation spell on me." I can hear the accusation in my voice, though I do not think it is her I really blame.

"I know." She sounds irritated. "Have you called me here, frail as I am, to discuss the undeniable facts of years past? Have your servants roused me out of bed for the mundane?"

And so I spit out what I have been thinking, what I want. "I do not want to die."

"Then don't." She laughs, rasping, almost inaudible. "Living and dying is your own business. No one else's."

I try to calm myself but I am maddened by her flippancy. I steady my hands and pour a cup of tea for each of us. I watch the small specks of leaves drift and settle in the cup.

"It is not so easy for some of us," I finally say.

She is very quiet. She does not reach for the tea. The steam from the cup twists around her wrists, like cloudy bracelets.

"And when my nephew is king, they will have no more use of me. I'll be returned to my room. I'll be shrouded in my sheets. They will wait for me to die." I try to catch her eye, but it is hard to do. "If they wait."

She shifts in her seat and the whole massive array of her robes and garments shifts with her like a separate animal.

"Waiting is a hard game to play at. I know. I'm waiting for you to get to the point."

"Help me." I am on the edge of chair. My hands are stretched out in front of me. I can see the veins and the knobs of my knuckles. They tremble slightly despite my best efforts.

"I do not have any magic for you." Her voice is softer now. "I have barely enough to keep myself together. I am old, so much older than you."

I nod my head, and now I feel that this was always the answer. I struggle to my feet, pushing hard against the arms of the chair. I nod my head again and leave the room.

***

I can hear the noise of the coronation from where I sit, hunched over the last breakfast I will eat as regent. The eggs are unappetizing. I pick at the toast with my fingers, letting crumbs fall on the tablecloth. One footman at the door to the room clears his throat in irritation, watching me. I ignore him. Eventually, he moves out into the hall, and I am alone. I can hear the tall grandfather clock ticking, its hands moving steadily—*tick, tick, tick*—around the face with the gilded numbers.

At last, I hear the shouts, the horns, the blaring music crescendo. Doors are opened and the noise wells up, loud, exultant, and then is cut off. The doors shut. There are footsteps in the foyer, the sharp clicking tap of dress shoes moving this way and that. The chancellor finds me. For the first time that I have seen, he seems relaxed and at ease, almost happy. There are still flower petals and confetti clinging to the velvet of his jacket. It makes sense that he would come, and not my nephew, the king.

"Thank you," he says, gracious in his triumph. "Thank you for your service."

I do not answer him. I push my plate away. It clinks against the glass. The chancellor holds his hands behind his back.

"The maids are airing out your room. You can return to the peace and quiet you knew before."

I stare at him. "I did not know anything before. How could I?"

"You deserve this," he continues as if he does not even hear me. "You deserve rest."

"I am no longer preserved."

He bends slightly at the waist. "No." I hear it then, the assurance that I might as well be preserved with all the guards and maids in constant watch.

"If I am to grow old, chancellor," I assume again the authority of a monarch. He widens his eyes slightly and his cheeks flush. "Then I will do so on my own terms."

"You are already old," he answers. "Don't be ridiculous."

I shove myself to my feet as quickly as I can. The chair screeches as it slides back.

"I shall decide when I am tired, chancellor. Or when I want peace. I will not return to silence and obscurity."

"You are not welcome at court." There is no longer any pretense of courtesy.

"Chancellor, I will not be imprisoned."

He blusters. "It is hardly imprisonment." There are guards who join him now, as if they had been waiting for a signal and grown impatient.

"Chancellor," I repeat, and I pull out the small pistol that I had held in my lap, tucked beneath the lace of my sleeves. I point it at him, and my arm trembles slightly, but it is steady enough to aim. "I will not return to that room."

The guards stiffen. They take a step into the room. The chancellor grabs the arms of the first man in. He grits his teeth. "Leave, then. You'll die soon enough on your own."

***

But I do not plan to die just yet. I take the steps down from my old room slowly, one hand on the stone wall, one hand clutching close the carpetbag with my shifts and skirts and pills. I find my way to the servant's entrance onto the gardens. The bushes crowding the door brush my shoulders and leave water in my hair. I can still hear the crowds from the front of the palace. They are singing and dancing, and I imagine for a moment that they are celebrating with me. *Long live the queen*, they shout in my imagination.

The garden walks are covered with small pebbles and they are slippery beneath my feet. I hold my arms out, finding equilibrium. I have not brought my cane with me. I trust that my legs will continue to grow stronger.

Perhaps, soon, I will even learn to run.

Winter Flowers

Alessia Galatini

Alessia Galatini is a writer and screenwriter. She likes to write the stories she's want to read (duh) and she's particularly keen on female-driven LGBT stories which aim to do something fresh and turn tropes up their heads.

SUMMER

San Francisco, July 1967

I see Persephone coming out of a psychedelic crowd of red and yellows melting together like flames coming to life.

"You really outdid yourself this time," she laughs, grabbing my hands and making me swirl around. "I hadn't seen anything like this since the Eleusinian Mysteries."

"They're not here for us this time, I'm afraid."

"Oh no, that's the best part."

And like that she's back into the crowd, dancing in different arms. With her long purple skirt and the flowers all tangled in her messy braid, she could easily pass off as one of these *hippies*. She shrugs off the centuries on her shoulders as if they were pollen. My daughter, my sweetest beloved daughter.

Come away with me, I want to tell her. Stay. It could be like this, always. But it's July already and every day when the sun is born hotter is a day closer to a cold, cold winter.

She's back with a crown covered in daises. She puts it on my head.

"If you're going to San Francisco," she hums.

"Be sure to wear some flowers in your hair," I finish for her.

"All across the nation such a strange vibration," she sings louder.

"There's a whole generation with a new explanation!"

People around us join in.

For a moment, I wonder if maybe this is enough to convince her.

"I told you they would learn, didn't I?" I say. "They want peace now."

"Yes, now. Mother, we've known them for thousands of years. It never sticks."

"But maybe if you'd help me we could —"

"I am helping you. Where do you think Hades is right now?"

I bite my cheek. We had gone long enough without mentioning Hades.

"Somebody has to take care of those bodies in Vietnam."

"They want to make that better!" I point to the people surrounding us. "They're trying."

She pulls me into a hug and I'm almost scared to hold her back. Her skin is always cold ever since she left me. She buries her face in the crook of my neck. She was born in summer too, although every day was summer back then. Her little hands reached for my neck in the same way. My summer child, my flower child.

"When I'm with you, Mother," she whispers. "I stop looking for a little while, but I can't pretend forever."

I nod in false understanding.

"But it's still early," she adds. "And we can rejoice with these rebel kids. We can love and we can cast away the shame in choosing who to love."

I pick up the implied cutting remark towards Hades.

"We can sing and we can dream of a better world until summer fades away and dreams will go back home. What do you say?"

"I like the sound of that," I admit, letting her drag me across the busy city's streets, each house growing brighter in colour as we pass them by.

***

AUTUMN

Rome, November 1929

They're calling it a depression. It's finally hit here too. The song of the birds is getting quieter by now. I see the starlings flying against the twilight, in large dark flocks. I can't help but think them slightly ominous. The Queen of Hades, worried about birds. Funny.

Autumn is the season of pomegranates. My mother doesn't know I still come to the ground sometimes, even this season. Pomegranates always taste better if you pluck them from the tree.

The best thing about progress is the irony of it. Apparently, pomegranate is one of the best anti-aging remedies. And we called it the fruit of the dead.

See, irony.

The worst thing about progress is that it's blinding. It's like a sugar rush. Once you taste it, it's hard to go back. To slow down. To question it. Sometimes you have to be stopped. Sometimes you just throw yourself off a building. Who am I to judge?

But something about this place just doesn't add up. Death is mourned, death is despised. Here, they're shoving it under the rug. They're pretending it isn't really happening. The people dying aren't the ones that are being seen. I talked to them. They all said how much they trusted the system.

A stray cat starts eating a dead starling near my feet.

I used to think my mother had all the answers. That was until I asked her about the withering flowers and she told me not to look at those. I slowly realised she not only lacked answers—she was creating most of my questions.

But I trusted her even so, and I overlooked the dead flowers for a very long time because of that.

I remember when I ran away and we spent our first autumn apart. I could hear her calling my name, all day and all night. But I was angry, for how much she had lied to me. For not wanting to explain why I had to be exactly who she was. Hades showed me the other side of the coin. Yet even those answers weren't enough. I had to find my own.

I cursed myself and ate the pomegranate seeds because I was scared of being stuck with her forever. I never told her. She still thinks I was tricked.

I no longer despise my time with her. I can see how it fits into what I've made of myself. She doesn't see that. She has her own answers, which make her overlook my choices. It's just the way the song goes.

The cat leaves behind a few remains. They'll be gone tomorrow, before anyone can see them. I wonder if the other starlings have noticed this one's missing, but they keep swirling as the horizon grows darker. I have a bad feeling about the future.

***

WINTER

Auschwitz, January 1943

It is impossible to walk without stepping on dead bodies.

Some of them are still twitching, like crumpled leaves with a breath of wind.

This isn't just death. This isn't balance.

Which god would ever demand this?

"Are you happy now?"

I haven't heard her voice in months but it stands clear against the stillness of the snow-filled field.

We shouldn't be talking. Not in winter.

"Can't you see what you've done?"

A laugh escapes my lips. It's bitter. It tastes rotten.

"Tell me mother," I say, pointing to a corpse just next to my feet. His ribcage is almost bursting through the thin layer of skin. "What's this good man's story?"

She leans down and touches him.

"He was a barber," she says, her tone dubious.

"Before that."

"He grew up in a two-floor house. He loved to collect insects. He—"

"Before that."

She finally pauses. I think she understands now.

"He was born." Her tone is defiant, unapologetic.

"So what exactly is it that *I* have done?"

The silence lingers.

The snow keeps falling over the pale bodies as if it knows it is the only burial they're ever going to get.

"Even right now, the ground is sucking on this water, desperately clinging to life," I say. "Growth hardly knows end. Maybe a flower that will bloom from this ground will be ripped off and offered in gift. Maybe that gift will lead to love and that love will lead to life and weren't we right all along to water a flower bound to be ripped off?"

My mother isn't looking at me. She's still reclined over the dead man, crying.

"Weren't we?" I scream. "Answer me."

But she doesn't. It is not usual that she wastes a chance to argue with me, but I'm wondering if maybe for the first time she's seeing just how much she plays a part in what she hates.

"You used to understand the beauty of birth," she says then. "I remember it. You would lay in the grass for hours, listening to all the life that was happening just underneath the surface. You were a flower yourself."

"Yeah, well, maybe I was always meant to be a winter flower. You never liked those either."

I start walking away. The snow cracks under my feet like bones being fractured. Like stories being ripped to shreds.

"I never wanted this for you," she screams after me.

"You made me to want this," I scream back. "You made winter flowers. You made *all of this*."

All this darkness, Mother, it's on you.

I don't say it, but it hits her just the same.

She doesn't stop me from going this time, and I don't know if I'll ever see her again.

***

SPRING

Athens, April 1999

I hadn't been up here in centuries.

The pillars have cracks in them and the bronze and blue linings have faded from the roofs of the temples. But it's not that different. Our acropolis is not gone. Who would have thought.

"Hello mother."

Persephone stands by the Parthenon, stroking a cat. She wears a yellow raincoat but the hood is down and her hair is soaked by the light spring drizzle.

"You're not using that jacket properly," I mention.

She shrugs. The cat shakes the water off itself and walks away.

"Don't you think it's weird how cats always hang around ancient sites?" she asks. "The Colosseum in Rome is just bursting with them."

"Maybe they can sense something."

"Yeah, maybe."

She seems serene.

"How was your winter?" I ask.

"Relatively calm compared to past years. Then again, if the world is really ending I'm sure I'll be making up for it..."

"Something tells me it won't."

I sit down next to her. We probably sat just like this, once upon a time when these buildings were brighter. I try to remember how it felt. The once upon a time that was us.

"Then again, they've gone as up and as low as they could. If there was ever a proper moment to end it..." I offer.

"But it won't," she confirms.

We'll just keep going. Round and round. I'll keep losing her and getting her back and she will never truly be mine. Maybe this is how the world ends. I let her go.

"Persephone..." The words are stuck somewhere inside. She's probably been longing to hear them. "You don't have to keep coming back. If that's not what you want."

She smiles.

"I stopped coming back for you a long time ago," she says then. I don't know whether this should reassure me or not. She takes my hand and leads me to the edge of the hill. Countless buildings spread towards the horizon.

"I know I never told you enough, but I'm proud of you." She squeezes my hand. "Yes, Hades is my home. I love listening to souls telling me their stories. I love giving them peace. I couldn't stand to do what you do: just create and turn my back. That's not me. Yet when it gets hard down there, and it has gotten difficult over the years— it helps me to see what those souls have left behind. It helps me remember we exist because of each other."

"Stupid me to think you were coming back for your old mum."

We laugh.

The drizzle washes the ground anew. Staring at the world from the ruins of our old empire, we are back to the gods we once were.

Maybe I'll forgive her one day. Maybe she'll forgive me. And when I miss her, I'll still meet her on the leaves about to fall. At the rivers' estuary. On the hills that swallow the sun. At the end of every story.

The Mothership

K. Bannerman

When she's not hunting monsters or uncovering secrets in dusty museums, K. Bannerman writes murder mysteries, ghost stories, and all manner of tall tales. Together, she and her partner manage Fox & Bee Studio, a production company on Vancouver Island, Canada. Visit www.foxandbee.com to watch their videos, or pop by www.kbannerman. com to learn more about her books and publications.

Kyana woke groggy. Her nose felt dry. A film of old sweat and dead skin cells covered her skin. She took a sharp breath and moved sluggishly.

Her body, reluctant to wake, was not her own. Her hands drifted down to her belly and discovered it to be swollen up like a beach ball, taut and stiff, heavy as a sack of sand. It was the alien sensation of girth and weight, not the hit of adrenaline to her blood administered by the hibernation pod, that made her breath catch sharp in the back of her throat and her eyes flash open.

"Don't struggle, love," said Gila's low, hypnotic, soothing voice. "Don't fight the sleep. Give yourself time."

But Kyana jerked her arms out so quickly that her elbows connected with the pod's glass walls. Pain roused her faster than the overhead lights or the needle prickling her arm.

"I...I..."

"Be calm," Gila continued, running her smooth dark hands over Kyana's clammy brow, and for the first time, Kyana heard the tinge of concern in the woman's voice. Fear, hidden under a generous helping of maternal calm.

Kyana tried to sit up but her body resisted.

"What's happened?"

"You slept the whole nine months," said Gila, "You'll have the baby soon."

This torso was not the one she remembered. When Kyana had curled into the pod, she'd been lithe and lean, one of fifty women chosen for the mission; now she was round as a berry, with her belly button popped and a line of dark hair leading from her navel to the shadows between her legs. "The procedure took?"

"For you, yes," said Gila. Tears shimmered in her brown eyes.

And Kyana noticed, right then, that Gila's stomach was as lean and muscular as it had been when they'd departed Earth, nine months ago.

"Oh! Oh!" Kyana said, still flustered, now shamed, "It didn't work for you? I'm sorry— "

"No baby for me, I'm afraid," said Gila. There were other women clustering into the ship's cargo bay, their faces gaunt and grey. Millie, and Olivia, and Su. "No babies for any of us. Only you."

Avril helped Kyana to sit at the end of the pod, and she ran her palm over the swollen stomach with reverence. "Only you."

Panic rose in Kyana's chest. They'd all slept the entire journey - all fifty of the women, committed to the mission - and to only have one child as a result? Her mind cast around for information. "How far out are we?"

"Less than a month to Titan," said Mela, the navigator. "You'll have the baby before we arrive."

"Then we'll start again as soon as we land, yes?" Kyana said to Gila with hope.

But a dark grumbling percolated through the group.

"Let her be. Don't burden her," said Millie, who always seemed crabby and sour, and was suddenly, uncharacteristically caring. "It's nothing, Kyana. Are you hungry? Let me get you something to eat—"

"Tell me what's happened," she demanded.

Gila took her hand, stroked her fingers. "I woke about three months back," she said, "There was a problem with the sleep regulator. I was miscarrying, so the pod pulled me out of hibernation."

Bird-boned Olivia, sweet and tender-hearted, gulped down her sorrow as she took up the story. "I've been running the diagnostics; the best I can figure, we hit a field of ionizing radiation. We hadn't foreseen crossing a comet's path, I mean, the odds are astronomical, but—"

"For some of us, the procedure never took," said Avril, holding her stethoscope to Kyana's heart, listening for her pulse before continuing. "And for some, it took but didn't last. We were in such a hurry to leave."

Kyana bowed her head, remembering the rush of boarding the ship, saying goodbye to everyone and everything as the L-bombs fell in waves, slowing the planet's rotation, and the atmosphere started to wick away into the vacuum of space. The ship had spaces and supplies for fifty women, as well as vials of genetic material from over a thousand healthy men; this would give the mission the best chance of success, of achieving the diversity required to start the human race over. The crew, highly trained and in peak fitness, knew precisely what they were doing. They had no illusions; their mission started the moment the world began to end. They'd prepared their whole lives for the apocalypse.

Of course, that didn't make it any easier to behold.

Space is fickle. One well-placed comet left a path of destruction, perfectly positioned to trip them up and throw out their schedule, to set off the hibernation pods and trigger a cascading domino of miscarriages. Kyana looked to Gila and said, "So you'll try again when we reach Titan."

But Millie shook her head.

"The samples are dead," she replied.

The women clustered together. Some held hands, others bowed their heads. Like a heavy weight pressing down upon her, Kyana realized the implications of Millie's words. The outpost on Titan was waiting for them to populate it, but the genetic material was gone, curdled into dead goo. There would be no second chances.

Kyana ran her hand over her stomach, and it felt like a stone.

***

There was no heartbeat, no motion, no kicking or swishing or flutters. Kyana lay for days in her pod, crying into the crook of her arm, until soft-hearted Olivia came to her side and told her to buck up, then led her by the hand to the airlock, and showed her the names scrawled on the doorframe in charcoal. *Mitchell. Wen. Augusta. Brent.* On and on the names went, thirty in total. Olivia pointed to one, and read it out loud.

"Stephan," she said softly, "He was mine."

They embraced and cried together, but then Kyana felt a little stronger, and realized she was not alone in her sorrow. She ventured to the commissary, ate beef stew, drank a little tea.

When Avril sat opposite her, she gestured to her motionless stomach, and said, "Can you do anything?" Avril had been trained as the ship's doctor, and knew all the secrets of the human body.

"Best to let it proceed naturally," she said, "We're two days out from Titan, and you'll pass the biological material any time now, when your uterus is ready."

The biological material. Kyana nodded. Cold, unfeeling words were better. Olivia had shown the danger of sentimentality; best to be stalwart and realistic about the outcome.

"It's heavy," Kyana said, "It feels like it's made of rock."

Avril laid her palm on Kyana's belly. "Have you heard of a lithopaedion? On rare occasions, when the fetus dies, the mother's body will cover it in calcium until it resembles a little rock. It's a way for your body to stave off infection, to contain the foreign tissue. You may have a stone baby, but it's your body's way of protecting you."

"I wish it would cover my heart in stone, too," Kyana said quietly. "What do you think will become of us, on Titan?"

But Avril's heart had no armor, either. Her chin trembled, and without a word, she shrugged, stood up from the table, and walked briskly away.

Their future was too dark to imagine, yet in her flurry of hormones, Kyana found herself drowning in visions of days to come, so vivid and engrossing that she could barely see reality through her dreamscapes. The ship would land, the crew would set up the outpost, Bella and Hilde would get the oxygen pumps on-line, Magda would fire up the generators, Su would use her engineering skills to tap into the rich resources of methane that would power their bubble of life, but all their efforts would only delay the inevitable. Years would pass, crew members would die. Eventually, one of the women would be remain alone; Kyana's terror grew in measured paces as she became more and more certain, she would be the last remaining scrap of human consciousness in an unfeeling, uncaring, clockwork universe. Alone in darkness. Alone amongst the stars. Only Kyana and her baby of stone.

A sharp knife-stab wrenched her from her thoughts.

"Oh, fuck," she thought in sudden agony, "It's started."

***

Labor stretched out, long and brutal. She was wheeled to the birth room and Avril guided her with meditative words, calm reminders to breathe, gentle encouragement as they strolled along the corridors between agonizing bouts of contractions. Nothing in her training had prepared Kyana for this trial. The rocking motion of her gait seemed to lessen the pain, but the contractions wracked her body, turned her inside out, set her spine on fire.

Over her own harried cries, Kyana heard the ship's thrusters hum down as they struck the smoggy, sulfur-yellow atmosphere of Titan, a thick nitrogen-rich soup that slowed their descent like treacle, and she felt the pressure of gravity push upon her innards, push on her twisting uterus, push on that cold unfeeling biological material. She clenched Avril's hands in shivering talons and channeled her grief into her bellowing, felt the noise of her mourning echo like an earthquake through the sterile chambers of the ship. The women came and went as their duties allowed, leaving kisses on her sweaty brow, bestowing offerings of cold comfort in the barren silence of their new home world.

Time lost meaning. During a gap in the pain, Kyana saw that Olivia was there, and Gila, too. Avril bent her head between Kyana's legs. "Almost there, now," she said. "Fully dilated. Push, my love, push."

And Kyana pushed as Sisyphus had pushed that boulder up the hill, eons ago, only to slide back again on the scree of loose earth. Push and slide. Push and slide. Push and—

A shuddering gush erupted between her thighs. Liquid splattered over the metal floor. Kyana tipped her head back as the tears flowed from her eyes and the blood flowed from her hips, and her exhausted breath whistled between clenched teeth. The pressure released. Gravity lessened.

"It's over," she exhaled like a prayer.

Only to be answered by a pitched, angry, determined cry.

Kyana looked between her bent knees to see that Avril had rocked back on her heels. The doctor held the baby up in her hands, offering it towards its mother, speechless.

The ship's thrusters gave a roar and the metal landing gear scraped against Titan's stony surface, and the child squalled and wailed, flailing tiny arms. Kyana curled up, mouth agape in disbelief.

"It's alive!" Olivia said.

Avril held out the infant, red-faced and hungry, in her trembling arms. As Kyana took the child in her embrace and pressed the demanding mouth to her breast, Gila said in hushed wonder, "It's a boy!"

Space Witch

Richaundra Thursday

When Richaundra Thursday (she/ they) is not daydreaming about temporarily spell-stealing the voices of her 8th grade classes so they will listen to directions, she is voraciously consuming books on history, philosophy, science fiction and fantasy, poetry and science, like an especially pretentious Kirby. She also enjoys such self-esteem shattering activities as cooking, playing video games, going to museums and spending too much time on Twitter. Her scribbles can be found in The Poet's Haven, Star*Line, Blossomry, Eye To The Telescope, First Line and Silver Blade.

All the best hexes are specific, ya float me? And she gives the best. She can fill your ears with every scream ever sucked, unheard, into the void. She can leave your filters completely spic-n-span and you'll still swear there's some danger-musty won't come out no matter how hard you scrub. If you really rust her grates, she can rot your hydroponics, and hooboy, will you be sorry then.

She don't charge much. Mind you, she gets most what she needs for cheap, 'specially after what happened to Lt. Mitchell.

He was running some side graff: harvesting 'shrooms growing on condensers, the ones closest to the ion cannons. Folk said those were special. Something about the radiation unlocking your soul and opening you to the stars as if we don't got stars enough other side a view screen. S'only reason I can figure she'd even approach 'im, given his rep. Nothin' you could pull up on the Link, mind you; for "sake of peace," bunches don't get written down. But civvies tried to draw his eye little as possible and more than one fresh faced lady recruit was…discouraged from joining his unit for health of their own body and soul. Just talk, as the higher ups might say.

Any case.

She came calling. Her fiber mesh cloak barely a rustle; face lost between filtration mask and solar shield cowl. All that was hers hanging from pouches and bags strung to her utility waistbelt.

I wasn't there so can't verify, mind, but most agree she asked all courtesy and offered fair exchange. But Lt. Mitchell didn't approve of her or anyone like her, who didn't fit their assigned bolt in the machine ship.

Had he just refused, that'd be that and barely count a tale worthy relaying on third-cycle vidfeeds. But Lt. Mitchell did more than just say no. He sneered and cajoled.

Threatened too, more like than not and sent her off with a cuff to the head for her troubles.

I doubt he thought much more of it after that, but sure as suns, weren't but few weeks later, Lt. Mitchell had the misfortune of being in the third bay engine room: the one they always claimed was more than a little squiffy, on account of it being the only bay to home both specimens of the green that seem so exotic out here in the blank, as well as a few leftover automata that didn't fit in the second bay pods.

Lt. Mitchell paid the rumors no mind. Just going through routine checks. I like to imagine him whistling, one of those happy tunes of sweet oblivion his kind always seem to know: those privileged with the surety that not only can all things be understood, they can be controlled. Specifically by themselves, of course.

Now I'm just a lowly maintenance monkey, no holder of high learning, nor secret wisdom of any stellar cults, so I can't speak to what happened next. But then again, if you can find some gravs-lagged fool what can, I will fork over a week of astroturf vodka rations: the type still illegal in some quadrants as unacceptably toxic. You know: the good stuff.

Where was I? Oh, yes, the untimely and decidedly un-TIDY demise of Lt. Mitchell.

When they found him, the succulents usually harvested to treat sun-blindness had already started blooming out of his chest, apparently mistaking his lungs for fertilizer. His face was a contorted hologram of pain, though admittedly, that might have been the effect of the vines wrapping around his throat, the ones they call 'Lovers Legs' when the Linneans aren't around. These lovers apparently craved a closer bond because they had reached into his screaming mouth as if to link up with the thorny flowers sprouting from his torso.

They still don't know where his eyes are.

As near as anyone can tell, one of the bots malfunctioned. Sealed the door and knocked the carefully controlled stellariums to the floor, scattering soil and precious green. Told me there musta been some kind of accelerant, maybe something the Linneans were trying out.

Only way they coulda grown so much, so fast. They shrug with the carefully calculated indifference of those actively hoping to never find uncomfortably real answers.

Any event, there was no evidence of a struggle. Just a quick blow to the side of the head and he was sharing the floor with the rapidly expanding foliage. Sensors in the room indicate that the rogue machine knelt down and indeed, when they finally over-rode the locks and entered, it was still straddling him, arms by the side of his head, waist joints bent in ways they'd never been designed for.

It took four doses of ATV before the electrician that jimmied the door open finally slurred that it looked to him like the bot had been leaning in to whisper to the planter box officer. He said it was the damndest thing because those models don't have vocal capabilities, just a soundbox for an alarm. But when they opened it up, the box had completely melted, like electrical fire had burned it from inside out.

No surprise, they took no chances and jettisoned that heap with the scrap next day.

Now I doubt much I gotta tell you, but Lt. Mitchell was liked by few and missed by none so no real great shock when his death was quickly written off as 'one of those things' and we continued our crawl through the blank. Those that knew, knew better than to ask questions and the rest didn't care.

No one ever said it was the witch, how could it be? But after that, folk what sell things not on the menuscreens, mind their manners and make sure she gets what she needs to do what she do.

Now the real challenge, friend, seeing as it ain't scrip, is trying to find her...

Necromance

Alyssa Striplin

Alyssa Striplin was pulled from
the mud of the Missouri River and
raised in Truman's hometown. She
is an MFA graduate from Minnesota
State University, Mankato and
Composition Instructor at Missouri
Western State University. Her
publications include stories in
The Molotov Cocktail, Blue River
Review, Midwestern Gothic, and
Bull: Men's Fiction.

Max needs a ride.

She says it's from work, but you can smell the whiskey on her breath. Makes no difference to you. You're happy to be her chauffeur, even if she never pays for gas and it's 2am on a school night. It's worth it to have a chance to be alone with her. You have been bewitched by her presence—the fried neon hair, the bony wrists, the silver ring hugging her pouty bottom lip—ever since you met her in Biology. You hope that with time, she'll see you as more than just the mortician's daughter—the one who sits in the back of class and only speaks up when no one knows the answer to a question about anatomy. That's all anyone can say about you, since working with your father keeps you away from most social situations. Max is the only person in school that talks to you; the only one brave enough to turn around and ask to borrow a pencil. From there, your relationship grew: you were desk mates; then you were lab partners for dissections; then you were co-authors of a book report on *Frankenstein*; and, eventually, you were her friend because you had the keys to your father's hearse.

So, when she asks you to make an illegal U-turn in the middle of the highway so you can go to Quick Trip, you agree. It's worth it just to see her smile, even when the headlights from the oncoming semi catch on her lip ring.

Max is dead.

When you are out of the ICU, the doctors tell you that the hearse was T-boned in the middle of the highway. Max died on impact—whiplash from impact damaged her spinal cord and neck. You imagine the gold crest of a dandelion popping off the stem with the flick of a thumb. You, on the other hand, were in surgery for several hours. You needed a heart transplant immediately; lucky for you, one had just become available. When you realize what this means, you taste something bitter on your tongue—you had been compatible all along.

Max is mourned.

Your father prepares the body, and he forbids you from seeing it before he closes the casket. Perhaps as punishment for what you did to the hearse. He won't allow you to go to the funeral either, but you sneak out while he aspirates a man who had drowned in the county swimming pool. In the cemetery, you hide behind a tree and watch Max's mother cry into her newest boyfriend's shoulder as they lower the casket. You worry you'll have to wait a long time before everyone leaves; surprisingly, the mother is the first to go. Everyone tosses a rose, picked up from the nearest gas station, into the grave before they disperse. The gravediggers make quick work filling in the hole, having buried so many bodies in a town plagued by meth lab explosions and overdoses. They've grown sloppy, too, because the dirt is loosely packed. It takes no time at all for you to reach the coffin; you get there before dark.

Max is heavier than she looks.

For you, it's not a problem. You've been helping your father move remains since you could walk. That's the life of the mortician's daughter in a town like this—motherless and bound to the family trade. Sometimes, you wonder if your father was the one who embalmed her. Right now, though, you are worried about getting caught. The sun has gone down and the light is still on in the mortuary, even though you know your father should have left by now. You hope that he just forgot to turn off the lights again, but you still hold your breath when you unlock the door. Inside, the metal table shines like a polished mirror.

Max falls onto the table with a loud thump.

Your pulse quickens, listening for footsteps on the floor above you. Nothing moves, and you exhale deeply. The tools you left under the sink are still there. So is the book you ordered from Amazon, advertised as being bound in real human skin, but as an expert, you know it's really cow hide. It was all you could afford. You hope this works like fairies—believe hard enough, it will be real.

Max is still wearing her lip ring.

That's all you can recognize, really, in the pale pulp that should be her face. Still, you do not hesitate. You get to work. Before your father said you would inherit the family business, you had planned on going to college to study art. As a child, you'd enjoyed making people out of mud down by creek running behind the house. You used sticks for their bones, stones for their eyes, and gravel for their teeth. *My friends*, you would say to you father, but he always made you toss them away, to melt back into the creek bed. Now in your senior year of high school, you take an advanced ceramics class without him knowing. Teachers often comment on your ability to capture facial expressions in raw clay. You use those talents now to push cartilage, bone, and flesh to recreate Max's face. The decomposing muscle does not cooperate, so you make compromises. A nose more flat than Roman; cheeks pinched between thumb and forefinger away from the sunken skull; eyes more hooded to hide empty sockets. When you finish, you are delighted to see that Max looks as she did during 8am classes—only half-dead.

The book has a diagram of the constellation you must draw on the ground with chalk. It also gives directions on the order the candles should be lit. In the center of the drawing, you place the necessary ingredients. The book specifies nightshade and bone marrow, but you settle for poison oak and a drumstick bone from a bucket of KFC, licked clean. The final step is easy—the pet shop in the strip mall was having a sale. In your right hand is your father's scalpel, small enough for this kind of sacrifice. The hamster bites your hand when you hold it down onto the floor. You close your eyes and bring the scalpel down. A scream erupts from your throat—the scalpel is stuck in the back of your hand. The hamster wiggles free of your grasp. Blood is still spilt, so you spit out the words of the incantation, hoping your backwoods accent doesn't flub up the Latin. When you finish, you hold your breath and wait. The candles burn down to the bottom of their wicks and leave you in the dark.

Max isn't moving.

You throw the scalpel at the open book and sob. Your palms press into your eyelids, smearing blood across your lashes. It was stupid to think this would work, but you got your hopes up anyway. You blame Mary Shelley for putting the idea in your head, but you did the book report—you know the moral of the story. This isn't how death works. You should know firsthand: no matter how much blush you put on a corpse, they are already dead, and no amount of makeup or dark magic will change that.

The clock in the upstairs parlor chimes ten times. Your father will be looking for you now, if he isn't already. You gather your tools and hide them under the sink. Behind you there is movement, and you remember you need to catch the hamster before you leave.

Max sits up.

It is exactly like the movies make it out to be—slow and dramatic. The fluorescent lights snap on and she lets out a terrified moan. You tell her it's alright and rush to her side. Her skin is leathery and has lost much of its pigment—some is missing all together. On the right side of her face, you can see her molars click together when she tries to speak. A slick, stiff tongue wiggles the silver ring on her lip. Her legs swing to the other side of the table, startling you.

Max stands up.

You feel your heart racing when her hollow sockets fixate on you. Her head moves up and down, sizing you up. She inches closer, holding out her hands. The bones in her fingertips press into your cheek. They move downward towards your chest and you move closer, wrapping your arms around her. Max presses the hole of her nose into your scalp. Your heartbeat is a marble falling down a thousand stairs. She moans softly; your cheeks burn with blood. Her face nudges yours, and even though you know it isn't right, you plant a kiss on her lips. How could you not? You are not as naive as your father believes—you have seen the movies, you know the signs. Warmth spreads throughout your body. Max presser her face against yours, her mouth open. This is your first kiss, so your tongue is lost. It slides across Max's teeth, tracing grooves in enamel until you become painfully aware that you are making out with a skull. There is a sharp pinch and a metallic taste on your tongue.

Max bites you.

You touch the corner of your mouth and expect to feel pain. Instead, you shiver with anticipation. Without restraint, you kiss Max passionately. She moans louder, pushing you towards the wall. You submit and forget that your father could be here any minute. You have waited so long for this moment that you will not let anything take it away. Max moves down your neck, the lip ring tickling your flesh. You shudder in delight when she nibbles again. You hardly notice the second bite. Or the third. Soon, your ribs scrape against the broken teeth inside Max's skull.

***

At your funeral, they will scatter your ashes across the ground near your mother's grave. Before he leaves, your father will spy something shiny on the ground beneath his feet. He will bend over and pluck a small, moon-shaped piece of metal from the dirt. He will mistake it for an earring, still intact from the crematorium. There will be dried blood baked into the surface, and he won't know which girl it belonged to.

Dragon Fruit

Izzy Varju

I am a Neuroscience student with three cats and too many books and I hope to get more of both. Since reading minds and teleportation aren't possible yet, writing about them is one of my favorite things to do in the meantime. I live in the land of Venus flytraps and wait for the snow to come.

The ship listed to the side as they tacked, the crew busy yelling and pulling ropes and cursing every swell of wind, until they managed to make the turn. The overcast sky sagged overhead like a sail in port, but the storm hadn't brewed just yet so Luisella didn't plan to bother with it until it became a problem. There were more important things to do at the moment anyway.

"Here, Mutsu! Look, you want it?" She held up a treat, showing it to the dragon who pranced on the railing in anticipation. A pause, just until his bright red eyes settled on the prize in her fingers, and then she tossed the snack behind her.

In a flash Mutsu scampered over her crossed legs where they were resting on a barrel; his claws clamped onto her shoulder for a brief moment before he launched himself after the apple seed. The seed disappeared into his maw and Mutsu returned to his perch with a contented stretch of his mouth, rubbing his pearly green scales against Luisella's boots.

"Better than those weird fish sticks you were eating with that duchess, right?" Luisella mused, watching him curl his tail around the banister to keep his balance.

"Captain! Ship to the west!" The watchguard's call reached her despite the sizable distance between the crow's nest and her lounging spot near the stern of the ship. It must have been urgent if Simmons had decided to bellow instead of whistle the message down.

Taking out her spyglass, Luisella leaned further back in her chair to gain a clear line of sight over the port side and glimpse the sails of the approaching ship. The vessel in question wasn't familiar but the blue flag at the top of its main mast was. Emblazoned with the golden skull and crossbones, the sight brought a small smile to Luisella's face. They had parted only a week ago--it wasn't time to have another date for at least a fortnight. Not that she'd mind seeing Knitty again, but it was highly irregular. They had a solid respect for one other's independence--the odds of running into each other by accident were almost zero considering their careful division of the territory surrounding the Isles.

"Hold our course. We'll see what they want if they can catch up to us."

Taking her seat again, she watched as the ship drew within a league of them. It was a large brigantine, the two square sails puffing out like the breast of a soldier. The figurehead at the front was painted in ostentatious shades of red and bronze. This wasn't Knitty's usual flagship, but perhaps she'd switched for a change of pace.

Luisella returned to her task of tossing seeds for Mutsu until the bow was barely three ship-lengths away. The sight of it distracted her enough to end up pegging Mutsu in the snout with her last throw, but she couldn't ignore the fact that Knitty would never approach their ship like this. For one, there was no friendly cannon fire. No barely heard taunts on the wind, threatening disembowelment as soon as they came on board.

"Make ready. We don't want to let ourselves get tricked that easily," she ordered Edsel, sending the first mate below-decks to prepare the rest of the men. She cocked her gun as the ship drew alongside them, heart freezing at the sight that greeted her on board the Golden Skull.

The motley host of sailors had been replaced by those wearing a simple uniform, the sigil of a rearing horse clearly visible on each crewman's chest. At the helm stood Knitty, her expression as stormy as the weather, while a man clad in bright red kept a stiletto leveled at her neck.

"Hello Lovely Luisella, I must say it's a pleasure to finally meet you." The man's voice was hearty and loud, the type of timbre heard at garden parties in a palace calling for a rousing game of cricket or egging the dogs on during a hunt. It fit him perfectly.

"And who the hell are you?"

"You may call me Captain Zara. Miss Nitika here has been enjoying my company for the past few days. She makes for beautiful entertainment. You've heard the sound of her singing, I'm sure," Zara said, a private smile tucked into the corner of his mouth.

Luisella leveled her gun, feeling Mutsu's claws dig into her calf as he started climbing his way to settle around her neck. His tiny breaths smelled of burnt cider as she sighted along the barrel at Zara's immaculate profile.

"Now, now. I think I have you a little outnumbered here. You wouldn't want to make a bad move." Zara tipped his head towards the main deck of the Golden Skull and a quick glance revealed the troop of sabered sailors ready to jump at a moment's notice. "How about this: you come aboard without any fuss and your crew go free. I don't need some band of reckless nutcases to share any spoils with, and you'd rather they stay alive, so I think we all have something to gain from this."

"And if I decide to just shoot you anyway? Knitty happens to be a competitor of mine, one less sea-slug in my way."

"I'd hazard you don't give the same treatment to all your competitors as you do to Nitika here. If so, I wouldn't mind a taste," Zara suggested lightly, scraping his gaze down Luisella's form as though weighing her on an unseen scale. His polite smiles were starting to grate on Luisella's own composure.

"You think yourself a competitor? The Isles are already claimed." Luisella could remember the fight that had erupted out of it, Knitty had her pinned to the cabin door within seconds but they'd figured it out in the end.

"I'm well aware. But I understand if you need proof of the seriousness of my intentions. Allow me to demonstrate." Zara drove the blade of his dagger into Knitty's shoulder, spearing her against him. The pained grimace that flashed across Knitty's face for a second was enough.

"I was going to try for her bounty but even if she dies it means I have, as you said, 'one less sea-slug in my way'."

"I get it," Luisella snarled and let her weapon drop from her fingers. A pair of Zara's uniformed men threw a rope across the gap as she approached the port side with a queasiness in her stomach. The swing over took barely a second, and the moment her feet touched the planking of the Golden Skull he pushed Knitty forward for Luisella to catch, though her hands were swatted away before she could hold her up.

"I get poked a little bit and you just roll over? Come on, where's that reputation you're always going on about?" Knitty asked, pulling herself to her feet with an iron grip on Luisella's elbow. Her black hair was knotted into a thick braid that hung down her back and her free hand was pressed against the wound, blood oozing onto her shirt despite her efforts.

"What's a reputation worth if my nemesis is dead?"

"Not much of a nemesis if you have to rescue me," Knitty retorted.

"What's this?" Zara loomed up beside them and snatched Mutsu from around Luisella's neck. His claws caught in her ear as he was dragged away from her, the scratches stinging from the force of his struggles. His usual chirps morphed into a high-pitched squealing, the sound sharp in Luisella's ears as Mutsu frantically writhed and squirmed.

"Stop!" She lunged toward him but Knitty's hold on her kept her from getting any closer without sending Knitty slumping to the ground.

"Ah, I've heard stories about this little creature. Stole it from a duchess, I believe." Zara held up Mutsu, grasping the little dragon by the front legs and leaving him to dangle from his arm like a sodden coat. "Pretty coloring, a rare shade of green if I remember correctly. But it's a shame it doesn't have any wings. I wonder if it can swim."

He continued his musings as he strolled toward the side of the ship while Mutsu tried to curl up into a ball with little success.

"It's not an especially useful animal, is it? Rough pirate lord like you're famed to be and you keep a pet that can be tossed overboard so easily." He flung his arm out over the railing, meaning to knock Mutsu away and send him flying over the side. Mutsu sank his fangs into Zara's thumb, clinging to his hand as he was almost dislodged.

"Even its bite can barely be felt," he said, laughing as Mutsu finally slipped and fell to the deck in a heap.

"Mutsu, good boy," Luisella murmured, watching closely as Mutsu shook himself off and regained his footing before scampering towards her. A heel came down on his flicking tail, Zara keeping him pinned to the boards.

"He really is a perfect playtoy, but he doesn't belong on the sea. The Duchess would be happy to have him back. He'll look wonderful on a studded leash," Zara mused. "Or maybe as a pet for her daughter. She's such a precious little thing; I hear she has plenty of dogs to have fun with."

He frowned as he inspected his finger. The bite had an odd purple bruise spreading from it and his breaths came in quick rasps, their pace increasing by the second.

"You're right," Luisella said, smiling at him when he looked up in confusion. "Mutsu used to be a duchess' pet-- he's an apple dragon after all. They make for adorable little rascals. Harmless unless you feed them the right thing."

"You fu-" He choked over his own words as he fell to his knees with his chest heaving from the effort it took for him to keep breathing. Mutsu scrambled out from underneath his boot and hid behind Luisella, his snout the only part of him remaining visible. Soldiers rushed from their posts at the rigging and the helm. Their unsheathed swords spurred Luisella to drag Knitty over to the railing where the rope still lay thrown across the polished wood.

"Mutsu!" She pulled Knitty close, her grip rough but at least she was sure she wouldn't drop her while they crossed. "This'll be a bit painful." Mutsu scrabbled up her coattails as she stepped up to balance on the banister, and before she could consider how likely it was they would end up in the choppy seas, she'd kicked off.

A shot cracked behind them, splinters of wood catching in Luisella's collar and Knitty's hair as they swung out and away from the Golden Skull. They crashed to the floor once Luisella let go, but what breath was knocked out of them was also what kept them down when the firing really started.

Whistling one piercing note, Luisella curled over Knitty's prone form and hoped Edsel had followed her orders. The ship erupted with sailors crawling from below-decks, armed in anticipation of a friendly skirmish; the sight of the bristling uniformed pirates on the other ship sent them scurrying to the cannons and sails.

"This is quite possibly the worst way we've met up," Knitty muttered, voice muffled from being pressed against Luisella's chest. "Not that I mind the view."

"I'll make it up to you on our next date. Someplace nice on land, maybe a café for once," Luisella promised, pushing Knitty up to lean against a tool crate. Peeking over at the Golden Skull, she was glad to see they were pulling away slowly but surely. The bullets had stopped as a shot from one of their cannons blew up the Golden Skull's aft deck and the sailors hurried to the mizzenmast that looked in danger of tipping. "No excitement, no danger."

"Sounds boring. But I wouldn't mind if there was less stabbing."

Not for the first time, Luisella was thankful she'd picked her flagship based on its speed. Even as the Golden Skull labored to gain wind to its sails, they were already clipping along at a brisk few knots. Once she couldn't see the figures milling around on board anymore, she allowed herself to look back at Knitty.

"You know the ladies love scars, right?" Luisella asked, motioning towards the ones that crossed Knitty's collarbone in jagged white lines on her dark skin.

"No, one lady likes scars. And even then, I don't think I'd call her a lady." Knitty prodded Luisella in the stomach when Mutsu jumped into her lap, nudging against her fingers until she gave him a scratch along his scales. "And here's the real hero of the day. Make sure you give him some tasty rat meat."

"I think he prefers his apple seeds," Luisella said as she stroked Mutsu's head lightly. Now that they were away from the commotion for the moment, her thoughts turned to more important matters.

"We need to discuss the elephant in the sea, as it were."

"Zara has more men. He mentioned as much during his... stay. My fleet's scattered to the winds, but he's already making bids for the rest of the Isles."

"Will you join me, then?" Luisella asked in one breath, knowing what she wanted the answer to be but keeping her hope as tightly furled as a docked ship's sail. Knitty stayed silent for several moments, her shirt slowly staining red down her front.

"Yes. I'll always be your nemesis," Knitty said fondly. "But we have a bigger fish to catch now."

Pulling Secrets from Stones

Beth Goder

Beth Goder works as an archivist, processing the papers of economists, scientists, and other interesting folks. Her fiction has appeared in venues such as Escape Pod, Fireside, and an anthology from Flame Tree Press. You can find her online at http://www.bethgoder.com.

This story first appeared in Mythic Magazine, June 2017

In the lakebed by the mountains slept stones full of secrets. Waiting memories. Dissipating memories. Rachel could feel the hum of them, their longing for closeness, pressing against her as the sun pressed down.

She slid down to the lakebed. Dust rose around her, obscuring her truck by the side of the road. The air stagnated, heavy and dry, baking itself into the earth.

Her memories were dying--the secret ones, the memories that let her touch the sky, the memories of how to cast a branch to find missing things, or summon a flower in her hand. All of her most important memories. Gone.

She pulled a geological survey map from her pack, jostling her water bottle and a squished peanut butter sandwich. Unfolded, the map stretched farther than her arms. Red marks showed where she had searched. Not much of the map was marked--perhaps half an inch.

Rachel hiked until she reached the edge of her last red mark.

She turned over a stone--memory shaped--then cupped it in her hands. Ordinary. The next stone was the same, and the next.

The lakebed stretched for miles, with huge cracks like fractals in the dust. Endless.

Stones, stones, stones. None of them memories.

Wind brushed past, and for a moment, Rachel feared that the woman in the mountains had found her. This close to the mountains, the woman could feel the land as if it were her body--the sweep of wind along mountain backs, the plants that thrust themselves through soil, the intrusion of sun into shaded spaces. The woman in the mountains had described this connection to Rachel, back when she had described everything to Rachel. Before the anger. Before the woman had discovered Rachel putting memories into stones. Before the rift that separated them as no mountain could ever do.

When Rachel looked up, only the sun was above her. Her relief was empty. Dry. As much as she feared the woman in the mountains, she wished to see her again.

And Rachel did fear her. The woman was like a crash of rain, an avalanche, soaking everything in her path. Unaware. But Rachel had come to love her wild kindness, her fierceness. The woman would mix the colors of the sunset beautiful and bright. She would send goats to look after the elderly, those who had no children. With a splash of soil and a whisper, she could cure sickness in trees, but never death.

The memory of the woman hung above Rachel like a dark sky, full and treacherous. Waiting.

Waiting as stones waited. Rachel grabbed another stone, rough and rounded. Ordinary.

She pulled the sandwich from her bag, wishing she had packed a more substantial lunch. Somewhere in the lakebed, locked in a stone, sat the secret of spontaneous berry pie. She remembered holding out her hands in the garden, a steaming boysenberry pie appearing among the flowers. But she couldn't remember how she'd done it, only that once she'd known the secret of it, when the lake was full, when water ran over the stones.

A crow circled overhead, dove, and landed on a boulder. "You'll never get anywhere that way," it said.

"No one asked your advice."

Of course, the only memory she'd found was the one that let her talk to birds. That memory stone was sitting in a bowl of water back at her apartment, submerged so that it would work.

"The way you are searching," said the crow, "so inefficient. Why did you store your secrets in pebbles?"

"I stored them in the lake." It was a good place for such memories. When the secret memories rubbed up against the regular ones--how to send a fax at the photocopy store where she worked, the amount of coffee to put in the machine, the name of the guy who ran the junkyard--the magic became duller. She couldn't hold everything in her head.

And the other memories--the secret ones--they would change her if she let them get too close.

The crow shifted from foot to foot. One of its toes was missing. "Call the memories back to you. Call them from the stones. Secrets once yours will find you."

Rachel shook her head. There was safety in distance. Such a memory would twist through the pathways of her mind, changing what it found there. She could not afford such closeness. She wasn't like the woman in the mountains.

"Fill the lake with water. Summon the rain," said the crow, as if such a thing were simple.

"We all want the drought to end. I would have done it already if I could."

"You insist on being difficult." The crow picked up a stone in its beak then tossed it away. "Talk to the woman in the mountains. She'll know where the rain went."

"She won't want to see me." Rachel grabbed another stone. Ordinary.

"Do not presume to know what the woman in the mountains wants," said the crow. "If you want your memories back, follow me."

The crow flew into the sky. It was headed in the direction of Rachel's truck.

***

When Rachel got back to her truck, the crow was sitting on the hood. It flapped its wings impatiently.

She patted the Toyota Stout, ignoring the crow. The Stout always made her feel better. Safer. Each part was known to her--valves and pushrods, radiator, gauges--all the parts that pushed against each other, all the parts she'd built into the engine. Solid. Logical.

She leaned into the truck's sturdy frame.

When she'd found the Stout in the junkyard, Rachel had been taking apart the engine of a Mazda Bongo van, just to see if she could put it back together. Across from the Mazda sat the Stout, just like the one her dad used to drive. The outside was rusted in spots, but it had a strong engine--salvageable. She'd spent her weekends working on it, until it ran right.

The crow hopped to the car door and pecked. "The trip will be easier while the sun is still out."

"She won't help me."

The crow pecked again at the door. "I'll show you the way."

She looked to the sky, hoping for rain. In the drought, she'd lost the best part of herself. Rachel had forgotten how to make origami cranes that dispelled heartbreak as they flew over the town. She'd forgotten the location of the singing snakes, and the name for the nettles that could mend anything--a sweater, a bag, a bone.

Rachel climbed into the car and opened the door for the crow.

The mountain road was twisty, unkept, full of potholes. Her truck complained, shaking when it went over rough patches. She could picture the engaged engine--every moving part--almost as if the truck were an extension of her body, almost as if its murmur were her breath.

The crow perched on the passenger's seat, uncomfortable. It opened its wings, knocking into the stones she kept on the dashboard. Memory-shaped, but without memories. Not yet.

The truck made a bubbling noise. A sign that it was overheated. Not good.

She pulled over to the side of the road and grabbed her tools. The crow perched on her shoulder as she lifted the hood. Before her, the beautiful engine hummed. It was like a living thing, like a beating heart. An old heart. Every part, she'd touched with her hands. Every part knew her.

Steam rose from the truck. She'd have to let it cool off before she examined the engine.

"Bet you wish you had your memories now. The mending nettles would be useful, yes?" said the crow.

"I'd never use magic on the truck."

She didn't need magic to repair the Stout. Truck knowledge was a different kind of knowing. As a kid, she'd spent hours working on her dad's truck. He'd shown her how to salvage the best parts from the junkyard--shown her what was useable, even if it didn't look pretty, what was truly gone and rotted through. "Take stuff apart. Use the crowbar. Don't be afraid to get dirty," Dad had said.

Rachel sat on the side of the road. The crow perched on a stump.

"We're not so far, now," it said.

Rachel brushed dirt off her sleeve. "I don't expect I'll say much, when we find her."

"Don't you have anything left to say?"

Their relationship had been an imperfect thing, complicated by distance, cobbled together through kindness. Mostly, the woman's kindness.

She had shown Rachel how to find memories--the secret places to look. It was like searching in the junkyard. She had to look underneath to see what was really there, to see the potential of things.

Even after two years, the soreness from their last conversation wasn't gone. When the woman in the mountains had found the memory stones, she'd been furious. "This is not as I taught you," she'd said. She'd told Rachel to never come back.

The crow cocked its head, waiting.

"She has a different way," said Rachel. The woman in the mountains believed magic was like breath, running through all of life. Magic infused her, absorbed her. The memory stones were an abomination, she'd said. Lifeless. Distant.

"Different from your way," said the crow.

Rachel pointed to the truck. "The Stout, I know how it works--every piece, every part. If something's not right, I know where to look."

"And you think magic is different?"

"When the woman in the mountains taught me to pull flowers from my hands, when the roots embedded themselves, when the stems shot up from my skin--" Rachel couldn't describe how she'd felt--terrified, yes, but alive. The flowers had pulled at her skin, grown from her body, part of her. She hadn't felt pain, but a pressure. Sunlight on leaves. Wind on petals. "There's no way to understand how it works."

"You keep a dangerous distance," said the crow. "You want to hold a thing without letting it touch you."

"Necessary distance."

The crow fluttered its wings, then settled. "Not for the woman in the mountains. Do you remember what she taught you?"

"The stones remember."

"You kept nothing for yourself?" The crow shifted, flexing the foot with the missing toe. Rachel wondered if it could still feel the toe, the place where the toe had been.

She'd kept nothing of the magic. That was gone from her. But there were other memories--ordinary ones, true ones. "I remember flying," said Rachel. "The mountains were sharp against the sky, but I wasn't afraid. Not with her."

"You could fly again. Call the memory to you."

Rachel thought of secrets bottled in stones. She would not call to them. The crow should not have asked.

The Stout was still steaming, but less now.

Rachel stood up. "The engine should be cool enough."

She leaned over the truck, hoping for an easy fix. Maybe a leaking hose. She revved the engine and watched the steam slide up. Not a hose--she could tell by following the flow of steam. She inspected the gasket. Not the problem. With trepidation, Rachel examined the radiator.

It was cracked.

She swore and gently closed the hood. They'd made it about three miles up the road, and the lake itself was two miles from town. The sun dipped lower in the sky.

She pulled a sleeping bag out of the truck and secured it to her pack. There was water, but no food. She hadn't expected to be out so long.

She could turn back, go into town. Come back the next day and repair the truck. Instead, she asked the crow, "How much farther?"

Rachel set out on foot, following the crow as it flew. She hiked for a mile over the winding road, until the crow flew over a side trail.

The trail twisted higher. At some points, it was barely a trail at all, obscured by rocks, covered by fallen trees. Not cleared in years--maybe not ever.

Although Rachel missed flying, it was good to hike.

The sunset lit the sky an intense purple. The crow flew down and perched on her shoulder, heavy. Talons pressed against her, all but the missing one on the left foot. They had to be getting close.

"The woman in the mountains. Can you tell me--" Rachel took a breath. She needed to know if she was forgiven. If there was a chance of forgiveness.

The crow said, "Koww, koww."

Rachel turned to look at the crow.

The crow cawed, again and again. She couldn't tell what it was saying. She asked the crow to fly up, to lessen its grip on her shoulder, but it didn't. It couldn't understand her either.

She'd lost the ability to talk to birds.

Rachel thought of her memory stone in the bowl of water on her bookshelf. Something must have disturbed it. The cat. Her roommate. The memory couldn't work out of water.

The crow hopped off her shoulder, agitated. It danced around, pecking at the ground.

"Tell me where she is," said Rachel.

The crow grew, bulging in odd places. A wing became an arm. Toes grew from talons, one missing.

The crow stood, no longer a crow, but a woman.

The woman in the mountains.

Her hair had changed since Rachel had last seen her--it had grown longer, more wild. The hair wove around the woman, braiding itself, clothing her. She was smaller than Rachel remembered. And her eyes were harsher, dark blue and intense.

"Now we can speak properly," the woman said.

But Rachel couldn't speak. She wanted to ask forgiveness. She wanted to argue. Rachel had forgotten the wildness of the woman. Quick breath. Fierce smile. That smile sang of the world the woman had introduced--a world of possibilities and rawness, a world of secrets. The words Rachel did not say fell heavy like the air around her, charged and compressed.

At last, Rachel said, "Your toe."

"Gone," said the woman.

"An accident?"

"What is one toe, when I have the mountains, and the little streams that run through? The plants that weave over rocky soil. The sky. The sun that presses down."

"You didn't have to hide." Rachel thought of the crow perched on her shoulder, its talons pressing into her. Stolen closeness.

"I wanted to see if you were the same," said the woman.

"I haven't changed."

"No, you are so frightened of change. So frightened that you trap secrets in stones." The woman cast a stone into the air. It burst into dust. "A lake is not a place for secret memories. Now it is dry. Full of nothing, not even water."

Rachel thought of the landscape, dry where once it had been green. She imagined animals and people looking up to the sky, hoping for rain. "I never meant for that to happen."

"A drought is caused by many things. Only some blame falls on you."

"But you still blame me," said Rachel. "For everything."

"When I showed you how to find these secrets, I did not know you would hide them. I did not know you would be so afraid."

"I can't do what you ask of me." The memories had a wildness to them, elements Rachel couldn't control.

"You must choose," the woman said. "The stones cannot live in the lake. You must take the memories as your own, or not at all."

As she spoke, the woman opened her hands. Two flowers grew, poking up through her skin. The flower in her right hand became larger, blue. The flower in her left hand red and glossy.

Rachel looked at her own hands, where no flowers grew. She looked to the mountains and the wild sky. "I can't become like you."

"You would give up magic? And for what? A life you do not like? Your old truck that doesn't run?"

Rachel thought of the Stout, the engine she had labored on so long, the way all the pieces fit together to make something greater.

Rachel clasped the woman's hands, bringing the flowers together. The stems twined and grew, latching onto Rachel's skin, weaving her to the woman. The flowers merged and became as purple as the sky.

"To build an engine--it's not magic, but it's not an ordinary thing," said Rachel. The flowers twined around her arms. "It's somewhere in between."

"For you, it's not an ordinary thing."

"If I take the memories, they will change me," said Rachel.

"You'll be as I am."

"Not as you are. But not the same."

"Change is constant," said the woman. A new flower crept up to the sun. "You were changed the moment I found you in the junkyard, turning over engines to learn their secrets. You were changed by all the moments in your life before, and all the moments after. Do not be afraid of change. Bite it. Take the secrets between your teeth. Learn. Pull the memories to you."

Rachel stood with the woman, twined to her, the whisper of flower pulling at her arms. The flowers grew and bloomed, twisted and branched. The sun sunk lower in the sky, until purple became darkness. But still, Rachel did not pull the memories to herself.

"Will I see you again?" asked Rachel.

The flowers disappeared. The woman became a crow.

"Koww, koww," said the crow. "Koww, koww."

Rachel thought of her memories, trapped in stones, trapped

where they should not be. She thought of flying through the evening sky, before the night had brought darkness, and the closeness of the wind. The weight of flowers on her hands. The crush of memory, a gentle wildness that pressed against her, but which she'd never held.

Tentatively, she pulled on the memory stone in her apartment, the secret language of birds.

The memory pried itself from the stone. Unbottled. Free. She could feel its pulse, like a new heart. It flew to her, over the dry lakebed, over the mountains. Home.

The memory submerged in her mind, awoken, alive.

The language twisted her mouth into odd shapes. Her thoughts reformed to speak in the language of birds--a mess of hunting, open sky, the night which leads to home or death.

With closeness came understanding, of a sort. But her heart was still a human heart. Undiminished. She felt as she had when flying. Unafraid, despite height and distance, despite the infinite sky.

"Will I see you again?" asked Rachel in the language of birds.

The crow who was not a crow flew up into the sky. The map in Rachel's pack leapt out and unfolded itself. A new symbol appeared, marking a spot in the mountains--two flowers twined together. A location. An offering. A way to find the woman again.

Rachel gathered up the map, then hiked down the trail until she found a sheltered space. The language of birds sang in her head, raw and wild, a part of her.

Miles down the road, the Stout waited for her, its radiator still cracked. Tomorrow, she would go to the junkyard and get what she needed to repair her truck.

Behind her, rainclouds loomed, blotting out the stars. A storm was coming.

Checkmate

J.S. Veter

Jessica's work had been published in New Realm Magazine, Beneath Ceaseless Skies, and by Seventh Star Press. Her novel 'Gateway' came out in 2012. 'Six' was published in 2016.

Umam Preth was preparing a deadly concoction of 3 parts jaffiger and 2 parts sillin when the robot slammed through the window.

"Hey, Professor," the Vee3 said. Its manipulator field rolled it upright.

Umam Preth watched the spilled jaffiger slip through the cracks of the plas-mesh floor. Without the jaffiger, sillin was only mildly noxious. It lapped innocently against the walls of the last martini glass in the universe.

"Physics have gone odd," the Vee3 said. "Have you noticed?"

Umam Preth swirled the sillin in the glass, then downed it.

"Offing yourself?" The Vee3 found a centre of gravity over the kitchen table and orbited slowly.

"Trying to, damn it," Umam Preth said. The sillin entered his blood stream, bounced around as if looking for something to do and then expired, leaving nothing but an ache in Umam Preth's many hearts. "You made me spill the jaffiger."

"Ah, was that the last of it?"

"Yes, it was." Umam Preth, his back to the shattered window, which as of this morning looked over nothing, put the empty martini glass on the cluttered counter. Allowing clutter was unlike him. His wife, had she been alive and not a gradually decomposing mass in the bedroom, would have been shocked. But, having been a compassionate sort, she would have immediately known that something was wrong with her husband. She would have put on soothing music and rubbed his dorsal hump. She would have poured him a drink far stronger and much smoother than an incomplete suicide cocktail.

Some more things to add to the list of things gone forevermore: music, back rubs and (Umam Preth burped) cocktails.

"Why are you here?" Umam Preth asked the Vee3. "I told you to stay out of my sight."

The Vee3 continued revolving. "I stayed away as long as I could," it said, "but what with everything so, you know, *gone*, there was nowhere else to go." The robot spun on its axis. "You could pretend you can't see me," it suggested. "You're very good at that."

Umam Preth growled at the robot. It had belonged to his wife. She'd had it since she was a child, had kept it in spite of its increasing obsolescence, in spite of Umam Preth's threats to replace it with something state-of-the-art. Hah. The joke was on him.

The Vee3 was once again the pinnacle of its kind. So, for that matter, was Umam Preth. Were his audience anyone other than a rusty AI with a broken loyalty chip, he would have announced--even as nothing pressed itself against the windows of his house---he was pleased with himself. The very same Umam Preth who'd been laughed out of the University Club for hypothesising that people had once lived in the ocean, and had finally, inarguably, achieved a position at the very top of the food chain.

Of course, these days the entire food chain consisted of himself, the Vee3, and a wizened apple he was saving for a special occasion. And his wife and her associated bacterial decomposers.

"How much longer do you think?" Umam Preth asked.

The Vee3 extruded its eye stalk."Five minutes, maybe?" it said.

"You can't be more precise?".

"I have explained this," the robot said. "It took three years for the outer system to be swallowed up, but twice that for the eastern hemisphere to disappear. Prediction is difficult."

What can you do with five minutes? Umam Preth must have said it out loud because the AI suggested, "Chess?"

Umam Preth groaned. One of his wife's attempts to endear him to the Vee3 had included programming the robot with the memories of 83 different chess masters. Umam Preth had never in 37 years won a game against the Vee3. The Vee3 set up the board. Umam Preth chose white.

"This is cozy," the robot said. It was a line Umam Preth's wife had used. Umam Preth could hear her tones in the AI's voice box. It should have soothed him to know that one small piece of her would exist until the end of all things approximately five minutes from now. Instead, it annoyed him that she wasn't around so he could complain about her robot.

His wife's decision to kill herself had been no surprise. In the beginning, she had born the end pretty well. They were together, she'd said, that was all that mattered. But she missed her Book Club more than she'd thought she would, and the daily trips to the market, which she'd loved, became impossible when the rest of the world went away. The streets were gone, she'd complained, and the last time she'd been to the baker there had been no sticky buns, even though he'd always saved some especially for her. Umam Preth had wanted to point out that there wasn't a baker anymore, either, but he'd bitten his tongue.

The Vee3 accessed its m-field and the game began.

Umam Preth's wife had been so interested in the world. All the small doings of friends and neighbours had been important to her. When they were gone, no matter how she protested that he was enough, Umam Preth knew she missed them in the largest cockles of her hearts. Hers had been the second suicide cocktail he'd mixed. The first had been tested on the neighbour's pet pooch. It had worked: the pooch, vomiting and dropping feathers, had stumble-fluttered to what it had thought was home but was, mercifully, nothing at all.

The third cocktail was the one the Vee3 had made him drop onto the plas-mesh floor.

Umam Preth supposed it was fair that he was the one left behind. It was his invention, after all, which had started all the ending. Best to witness it himself, scientist-fashion. He'd have taken notes if he could. He had his books, but there wasn't a pencil to be found between here and, well, right over there.

With a sucking noise, the nothing moved into the house. The Vee3 announced its entrance as if announcing a dinner guest. Umam Preth, losing three pawns in quick succession, barely looked up. But when the nothing removed his wife's remains from existence, he banged his flipper on the table so hard it hurt.

"Look on the bright side," the Vee3 said in his wife's borrowed tones, "it works."

Which was the very thing the woman herself had said to him

the night astronomers from seven different countries arrived at the same terrifying conclusion: galaxies were disappearing from the heavens and the epicentre of the phenomenon was, however unlikely, Umam Preth's kitchen table. His wife had looked at him with surprise. She'd told him for years that someday one of his inventions would work. It wasn't until the day one actually did that Umam Preth realised she hadn't believed it at all.

Umam Preth had frowned at the glittering box and its flashing lights. "It's not supposed to do *that*," he'd said, fiddling with a dial or two. In retrospect, fiddling with it had not been a good idea. It was most likely the fiddling that had activated the failsafe.

Umam Preth vaguely remembered installing the failsafe after a few too many, but (as with so many things that happened when he was drinking) he was stymied as to how he might uninstall it.

"What's it supposed to do?" his wife had asked.

"It's for your birthday," Umam Preth explained. "A new waste disposal to replace the one I broke."

"That is sweet," his wife said, kissing him. "How thoughtful. All the same, dearest, perhaps it's best you turn it off now."

"Seems a shame," Umam Preth said, "seeing as how well it's doing... whatever it is it's doing."

Unfortunately, it appeared Umam Preth had neglected to include a kill switch when he'd installed the failsafe.

Still, they'd had decades. The universe was mighty big and the machine, though tireless, wasn't. Umam Preth placed his invention on the kitchen table. His wife draped an embroidered cloth over it so it fit in better with the decor. Umam Preth went back to teaching. They considered getting a pooch. Stars grew few, then none, save their own sun. It got very bad for a while.

"You'd better make a move," the Vee3 said. There had been a long silence between them. The only light came from the Vee3's battery warning and the last glow of the universe, which powered Umam Preth's machine. The robot had captured Umam Preth's castle and knight without effort.

"I think now's the time," Umam Preth said. The Vee3 adjusted its m-field and the wizened apple, the very last apple in all of space-time (which was now jammed into Umam Preth's cramped, cluttered kitchen), deposited itself in Umam Preth's hand. "I never liked these," he observed, turning the fruit. Its skin had gone wrinkly like Umam Preth's face. The apple had ripened last summer on the tree in their back garden. His wife had made pies and sauce from most of them, but this one had fallen forgotten into the back of the fridge and waited there until everything else had been eaten. Umam Preth turned it over, realised that this apple was the last sunlight of the world that was. He sniffed it. It smelled like fridge. He took a bite. The skin parted under his teeth. He chewed, swallowed and found he still didn't like the damned things. He finished the apple, core and all, until all that was left was the stem and one tiny shrivelled leaf. He tossed those to the floor.

The nothing would take care of the waste soon enough. It had pressed into the kitchen, swallowed the cooker and the empty, powerless fridge, taken the pictures on the walls.

Then Umam Preth saw a chance: three moves, clear as his eyesight was not. The Vee3's battery indicator blinked at 'low'. Umam Preth hardly dared to breathe. Casually, he made his move. He had been here before. Once, he'd gotten within two moves of winning before the robot had cleared the board with a savage attack.

Then it happened.

The Vee3 *placed its rook exactly where Umam Preth wanted it to.*

"My turn, then?" Umam Preth said, voice cracking over the question. He double-checked the pieces on the board, making sure there wasn't a trap laid out for him. There was always a trap.

Umam Preth's hand hovered over his bishop. He didn't see a trap. Didn't mean there wasn't one there. "Still my turn!" he said, pretending to ruminate. The Vee3 sank slowly to the table, its light blinking red. Please, please, please! Umam Preth thought.

The nothing lapped across the kitchen floor, its pulses matching the hum of Umam Preth's invention. He sank lower into his sling, made his move, held his breath. He had to be missing something. He'd been playing against the Vee3 half his life. He'd never won. Not once.

The Vee3's m-field was sluggish. Its knight crept across the board. Again, right where Umam Preth wanted it. Umam Preth was going to win.

Umam Preth twitched his right flipper away from the nothing. He was going to beat the robot at last! What a way to go! This was even better than when he'd beaten Professor Zsen Eb five out of seven. *Ha!* Who had tenure *now?*

His chair tilted suddenly as the nothing took its back legs. Umam Preth stood, pounced on the robot's king. "Check and mate!" he exclaimed. "Check *and* mate! You didn't see *that* coming, did you?" The Vee3 settled to the table, its lights dark. "Wait," Umam Preth said. He scanned the board; it looked like checkmate. Yes. Yes! Yes? "You didn't just let me win, did you?" The table lurched. Umam Preth saved the game board from toppling to the floor, stepped back from the nothing's gobbling. "You weren't just being nice, right?" He pointed an accusatory finger, but the little robot was gone.

"I won, didn't I?" Umam Preth asked all that was left of the universe. "I won?"

A Dream of This Life

Andrea Blythe

Andrea Blythe bides her time waiting for the apocalypse by writing speculative poetry and fiction. She is the author of Your Molten Heart / A Seed to Hatch (2018) a collection of erasure poems, and coauthor of Every Girl Becomes the Wolf (Finishing Line Press, 2018), a collaborative chapbook written with Laura Madeline Wiseman. She serves as an associate editor for Zoetic Press and is a member of the Science Fiction and Fantasy Poetry Association. Learn more at: www.andreablythe.com.

The shadows are thicker than they should be. They fill up the corners of the room, pool under the crate that serves as a TV stand, nestle into the discarded clothing and wadded up fast food wrappers on the floor. They seem to churn with hidden creatures; hairy legs climbing over shiny carapaces.

I press my palms into my eye sockets. When you haven't slept in weeks, life takes on a grayed-out vibrancy, a too-vivid blurring of the ordinary.

All I want is to lay back and slip into unconsciousness, but I don't bother. No point in spending the rest of the night staring at the cracks in the ceiling until the morning's sickly light sneaks through the curtains.

Eric, professional panhandler and my sort-of boyfriend, shifts in his sleep. I watch the flicker behind his eyelids, the slow rise and fall of his chest, and hate him. The hate is so intense I want to weep or scream or kick him off the mattress onto the floor. I have a brief vision of grabbing a butcher knife from the kitchen and prodding him awake with it. What color would the blood be in the near pitch black of the room?

But I shouldn't be such an ungrateful shit. Eric has been letting me crash in his tiny studio for months without paying a dime.

Even before I started sleeping with him. As of late, my own method of income has been, to put it lightly, sparse, and it doesn't look like it's going to get better anytime soon.

If I could only sleep, or better yet, plug in a few diodes and a heavy sedative drip, I could get back into the dreaming scheme of things. Nothing beats a good drug-laced dream, especially if you get paid cash under the table. Life would be shiny and bright, instead of this series of stretched out empty moments and me just begging my body to please, please give into exhaustion.

I pull my feet up onto the mattress, tuck them under the end of the blanket, protecting them from the reaching shadows. My eyeballs feel as though they are made of sandpaper, my limbs are rubber. The shadows are nothing but empty air, places where light doesn't reach—but I can feel their growing intensity.

Snatching my phone, I force the darkness to retreat with the dim glow of its screen. The shadows will reconverge eventually. No point in sitting there waiting for them. No point in sweating over sleeplessness, so I jerk on a pair of jeans and a sweater, shove my feet into flip-flops.

Eric grins in his sleep, slumbering like a princess on a feather bed waiting for true love. I could kiss him awake, let him wrap his arms around me, nestle and comfort me, but I don't. I just stand there considering the scab on his chin, the one he got when I nearly passed out on the street a week ago and he slammed himself into the knot of a tree trying to catch me. He doesn't wake as I grab a handful of his cash and disappear out the door.

***

No one wants my dreams anymore. This has been made abundantly clear by the weightlessness of my wallet.

When I first started dream selling, I could conjure richly-textured fantasies, make myself a knight charging into battle against a towering, heat soaked dragon. I could grow wings and fly through fantastical landscapes; immense forests of impossible heights, craggy luminescent hillsides, flaming orange deserts, all in pursuit of adventure or treasure. My erotic dreams could steam glass with their sweat-soaked pleasures. Even on bad days, I could offer nightmares, the near threat of violence, the flash of a gleaming knife, the desperate flight, the thick-as-mud air preventing you from fighting back...not as desirable to the general public, but still valuable to a certain subset of clients.

Now, the most I can summon are blank anxiety dreams, denying anyone the joy of wonders or the thrill of true horrors. No one wants to buy a dream that leaves them with the same unsettling boredom they experience every day of their lives.

I've stopped complaining to Eric about this, because he only says, "you should stop selling."

As though it's that easy.

He says things like, "I've read that the side effects can be really bad." And then he lists them: waking hallucinations, insomnia, violent behavior, suicide.

As though I don't already know this. As though I don't know that it's the dream selling itself that has screwed me. As though I haven't been to a hundred facilities, all of which lace the sedatives with a little hallucinatory additive in order to get a vivid digital file for replay. As if I don't know I've become so dependent on the additives and diodes and machinery I can't fucking sleep without it.

He keeps trying to fix me with bottles of melatonin and

over-the-counter sleep aids—always sending me articles about former dream sellers who turned over a new leaf through diet and positive thinking. He seems to have an endless supply of recommendations for psychologists, therapists, hypnotists, reiki practitioners, or whatever quacks out there in the world are claiming to have the secret cure to insomnia.

He's even recommend that I plug into someone else's dream, even though neither of us have the money and that's not really sleep anyway. The experience is more of a half-awake sequence of sensations that leaves your body tingling. Nowhere near the immediacy or control you have when you're selling.

I would be more pissed at his glut of nonsense, except he is obscenely sincere. In the end, he's the only thing that comes close to soothing me on the bad days, the days when I can't even sit still and I'm twitching from the need to sleep. It's something about the way he pulls me down onto the bed and just holds me, fingers stroking the back of my arm while I rest my head on his chest, feeling the rise and fall of his breath and listening to the deep rumble of his voice as he talks— nothing important, just a stream of stories from his day spent panhandling, talking until his voice fades out and his breath deepens, until sleep sneaks up on him.

When Eric holds me like that—even when he leaves me awake and alone in the dark—I can keep it together for a little while. A week sometimes, maybe two. But the exhaustion always shape-shifts into desperation and eventually I'm on the streets again hunting for a place to sell.

He always notices. There's a weight to his sigh every time he realizes he hasn't saved me again and he can't stop me from doing what I need to do. "Just be safe," he says, by which he means: use a legit facility, one of the clinics or a hospital, where you lay down on their crisp, white beds and record nice, clean, hopeful dream files; the kind of files used for medical and psychological treatments. He wants me to go to the kinds of places where they make you fill out forms and track your dream donations, where they restrict you to the medically recommended limits of no more than two sessions a month, at no more than six hours a session.

All overly cautious bullshit if you ask me.

What Eric doesn't understand is that even the less-than-legit facilities are unlikely to take my dreams at this point. Despite their reduced limitations—being practitioners of pleasure, instead of care—they still want dreams that are vivid, those fast, slick, juicy fantasies of action and horror and lust. The less-than-legit places value raw emotion over detail, and they'll demand a brain wave measurement to make sure they get it.

What I need is even more underground than the underground. In other words, what I need is any fucking facility that will take me.

Such places exist. I heard about one of questionable safety and cleanliness from a tenuous acquaintance in the dream-selling world. Sketchy is an understatement in describing his directions. I doubt he's even been there himself, but with everything blurred to the gray of a dingy window screen after weeks of sleeplessness, I'll try anything.

The metro hums around me. As I travel deeper into the city, with no clear sense of where I'm going, the buildings grow up like a dark forest around me. I press my forehead against the glass and lift my hand to block out the bile-yellow light.

***

I get lost in a maze of alleyways, stumbling over large, reeking garbage bags piled under broken street lamps. My feet, slippery with some unknown liquid, slide around in my flip-flops. I witness not one, but three drunk men bend over and vomit violently into three different refuse-cluttered gutters.

My phone buzzes in my pocket and I answer out of habit.

"Where are you?" I can see Eric rub the sleep and annoyance from his face in the brief moment before I switch the phone from screen to voice-only mode.

"Out," I answer and turn into a blind alley with bare, grubby walls. It's the wrong alley, so I backtrack to the street. A multitude of shapes shift in the deep shadows as I reach the corner. My heart thrums in my chest like a rabbit's. I'm not sure if there is actual danger or if I'm just hallucinating.

Either way, I should have brought the butcher knife.

"I know what you're doing," Eric says.

"Then you don't need me to tell you."

My phone pings with a request for video access. I click decline.

"I thought you said you were done with this. With all the...I don't know, dream crap. I thought you said you were done and that you never wanted to go back to all that, that you—"

"Do you have any idea how long it's been since I've slept?"

"Come home," he says. "Just come home and we'll figure this out. We'll fix it."

Home. Eric says the word with such hope. He says it like he's that Dorothy girl in that reel he loves, all longing and sweet. Every time he watches her, as she squeezes her eyes shut clicking a pair of glittery red heels, clicking and believing magic will get her home, he turns to me smiling like he's all lit up inside, smiling because when she wakes up, she'll be back with her family at last.

He speaks again after a brief pause. "I love you."

I know this conversation. I know exactly where it's going. He'll say, *why are you doing this?*, and *I love you*, and *please*, and I'll say *just one more*, and *I'm sorry*, and *I promise*. How many times have we had this conversation? How many times has it lead me back to anywhere like the home he imagines?

But the real question is: Why would Dorothy, or Alice, or Wendy, or any of those girls in blue dresses want to return to a drab, monotone reality when they could have the vibrant dream of another world?

"I'm not sure what's worse," I say, just wanting this little chat to be over already. "You saying you love me, or that you believe it."

Eric grunts like I punched him in the gut. "Goddamn, you can be mean."

Yeah. Fucking mean and awful and vicious. All rising up out of the nest of anxiety in my chest like wasps as I search for words that will let me get on with what I need to do. I say, "You're only want me back because you pity me, and because you're lonely, and because I fuck you sometimes."

"Fuck off. That's not true."

"It's the only true I know," I say. "Everything else is bullshit. Home and you and me. It's all bullshit."

He huffs again and says nothing. The silence stretched out while I imagine the shadows churning like snakes around my head. Then a pair of beeps signals the end of the call.

I lean against a grimy wall and rest against the cool plaster. Somewhere deep down inside of me is a mountain of guilt, surrounded by a sea of self-loathing. There's sadness in there too, and regret, loneliness, and loss. All mixed up in a general sense of shittyness. I'll pay for it later. It will all come reeling up to consume me, but for the moment, every feeling I have is muffled by so much exhaustion that I can't bother with any emotion other than tired. I could sleep here, just standing up and leaning here against a filthy building on who-knows-what street—if I could sleep at all, that is.

After a moment, the smell of piss wafts up from the concrete, so I shove myself off the wall and continue on.

***

By the time I find the faded, peeling green fairy sticker stuck to a plywood door, the sky is beginning to lighten into the coppery hue of a smoggy city morning.

I knock and inform the bulky beast of a doorman what I'm selling. He leads me into a large, bare room with stained, floral wallpaper and nubby, shit-brown carpet, which smells faintly of mold and old grease. A scarecrow in a brown suit sits in the center of the room behind a foldable card table, sorting a tower of paperwork. I don't remember the last time I've seen so much actual paper. He doesn't look up when the beast and I enter, or when the beast leaves without saying a word.

I'm not sure I'm in the right place. Most facilities, even shady ones, have some show of buying and selling. There are projection devices for buyers wanting to plug and play dream files. There should be beds, medical equipment, and recording devices for sellers. None of that seems to be here, but what the hell do I know. Maybe this is the reception area.

I clear my throat.

Scarecrow slides a piece of paper off the top of a stack, scans what's written there, places it on one of the other piles.

"Excuse me, I'm here to sell…" I pause, uncertain.

The man hasn't even acknowledged my presence yet.

"Sell what?" he says, not looking up. He shifts another paper from pile to pile in a slow, carefully orchestrated maneuver of his thin long limbs.

"Dreams." I chew my thumb.

The man sighs, a long exasperated sound like the hiss balloon deflating. He reaches under his table and pulls out a giant book, similar to the old-fashioned things hotel receptionists used in old movies, and flops it down. The table groans under the additional weight and the paper stack sways, nearly topples.

He produces a pen and opens the book at around the halfway point. "Name?"

Who cares in a place like this? I answer with the first goofball thing I can think of, "Aurora Borealis."

The pen scratches along the yellowing paper. "Date of birth?"

"The day the Earth stood still."

He lifts his gaze, scans upward from my dirty feet and flip-flops, over my jeans and tattered sweatshirt, to look me in the eyes. His expression is humorless and he looks more like a raven about to peck my eyes out than the scarecrow.

I meet his cold stare. "What the hell do you care?"

A hard-edged silence falls between us. When it's clear he isn't going to budge, I toss out a date that's close enough.

He writes this in his book. "Do you understand the inherent risks involved in this procedure and the fact that this facility will not be held responsible should any misfortune befall you, up to, but not limited to, death?"

"Not limited to?" I ask. "What do you mean 'not limited to'?"

He locks me with his sharp gaze again. "Do you understand the risks and assume responsibility for any liabilities involved?"

I roll my eyes. "Yeah, shit, whatever."

Scarecrow makes a checkmark in an unlabeled column, then turns the book around and holds the pen out to me. "Please sign here."

I take the pen, then stop, trying to remember the name I gave him. I settle for an illegible scribble, then drop the pen into the center crease of the book.

The man leads me through a door at the back of the room and down a long silent hallway of doors. He picks one and ushers me through. The tight, tiled room barely has space for the the two of us and a single, depressing gurney. The sheets are threadbare but bleach white. The sleep monitoring and recording equipment is outdated, but looks in good repair. The room smells strongly of ammonia.

I almost laugh in relief.

He gestures to the bed with his thin, awkward limbs and I climb on, kicking my sticky flip-flops to the floor. The mattress is a bit lumpy, but a few hours on it will be livable. I roll my shoulders and force myself to relax.

He attaches a number of pads with some sort of sticky jelly to my forehead, temples, and behind my ears. I watch him make adjustments and fiddle with the machines. The familiarity of his movements—which I've seen a hundred times before in a hundred other white rooms—is comforting.

The swab of rubbing alcohol on the back of my hand is cold and swiftly followed by the sharp prick of a needle. As the sedative hits me, my limbs loosen, my chest eases, and I can finally breathe. Already the tingle of receptors lining up with the diodes begins to soothe me.

Everything's going to be okay. I screwed up with Eric, but I can fix it. After I leave here, I'll be able to handle shit again. I'll give Eric my apologies and kiss away his hurts. I'll let him help me the way he wants to help me. I'll let him take me to a rehab clinic or whatever. I'll get off the selling scheme and I'll get a legit job as a waitress or a telemarketer or something. I'll let him love me and everything will be okay.

But first, just this one last dream.

The Ghol

Rose Strickman

Rose Strickman is a writer and all-around fantasy nerd living in Seattle, Washington. You can find her stuff in the e-zines The Lorelei Signal, Luna Station Quarterly and Aurora Wolf, as well as the anthologies Robotica, After Lines and Sword and Sorceress 32.

"Is the ghol coming back tonight, Mama?" Violet asked anxiously.

Miranda continued pouring her daughter a drink. "Probably, Violet. But don't worry: we still have lots of Papa's poems left."

Violet huddled around herself in her chair. There were dark shadows under her eyes, and her golden skin looked sallow. These last few months had been particularly hard on her. "I wish it would go away."

"Me too, honey. But wishing won't make it leave."

"If Papa were here, he'd kill it!" Lily slashed with her spoon, eyes shining.

"Careful, Lily." Miranda moved the jam out of her reach. "We can't afford to waste any food. And you can't kill a ghol. It's already dead."

Violet shivered at the thought, pushing food around her plate. "Where did it come from?"

That was the question that tormented Miranda, night after sleepless night. "I don't know, honey. But as long as we have Papa's poems, we're safe."

Neither girl said anything to this, and even Lily looked subdued at the inevitable conclusion: eventually the poems would run out. And then what would they do?

After supper, Miranda and the girls washed the dishes, hurrying as twilight welled up in the trees and spread across the harvested fields. Miranda rushed the girls through their chores, making them sing loud, cheerful songs and keeping them away from the windows.

She herself risked the twilight to lock the chickens safely away and ensure that the field 'tons had stowed themselves in the barn. They had only three field automatons left. She looked them over carefully by the hard light of the alembic coils. She did all she could to keep them in good shape, but with no way to get more parts, their eventual deterioration was inevitable.

Just like us. She stifled the thought and hurried back indoors.

The girls ran to her; they must have been watching through the windows. "Are you all right, Mama?" Violet asked anxiously.

"I'm fine, Violet. Stop fussing. Now. Who wants a story before bed?"

Miranda tucked her girls up in the big bed she used to share with James, while outside the light died away.

When she had finished with stories and both girls were asleep, Miranda flicked the switch on Rover's neck. The dog 'ton's eyes lit up. "Guard," Miranda ordered, and the 'ton began pacing back and forth, monitoring the room. If anything other than Miranda or the girls appeared in its sensors, it would set upon that creature immediately, be it a rat or a man. No doubt it would try to take down the ghol too, when the time came.

Miranda, meanwhile, went downstairs. By the door, she picked up an old, worn notebook left by the doorway for this purpose. There were many pages missing, ragged edges of paper stuck to the cracking spine.

Outside, darkness had fallen completely. The wind hissed through the trees, moaned across the fields. Miranda stood on the doorstep, a tall woman with hair and skin as dark as the night, her worn calico dress swaying in the breeze. Waiting.

Slowly, a white light grew in the woods: faint and faltering at first, darting behind trees. But it soon grew bolder. An eerie whine developed above the voice of the wind, and the ghol stepped out of the woods onto Miranda's land.

It was in the vague shape of a man, tall and formless, with too-long legs and arms. Two eyes burned in a featureless face. It began to move: walking counter-clockwise around the house, each circuit bringing it closer. Miranda stayed stock-still, waiting for the completion of its third circle. All the while, the eerie howl grew louder.

She saw it approach from the right. Closer, the monster seemed even worse than before: there were spectral organs moving inside it, the flow of insubstantial blood. The soil crunched under its feet.

And—*now*.

Miranda tore out one of the inky, ill-scratched poems her husband had written for her, tore it from the notebook and, crumpling it, tossed it into the wind. There was a flash of light—she heard, fleetingly, James's voice—and the ghol gave a cry that made the hairs on her arms stand up.

Then it was gone, as though it had never been.

Sighing with relief, Miranda went back inside. She bolted the door and leaned against it. Safe—for another night.

Moving by feel in the dark house, she thumbed through the pages of the notebook. There were only twenty left.

***

The next day dawned, gray and gloomy. Miranda knelt by one of the field 'tons, cleaning its cooling vents. Despite everything, she couldn't help taking pleasure in mechanical craft, even something as basic as 'ton maintenance. This had been her joy since she was a girl.

Nearby, Lily watched, fascinated by Miranda's work, but Violet kept glancing out the barn door toward the fields and the trees beyond. "Is the ghol still there?" she asked.

Violet really was too thin, Miranda worried, squinting at her in the glowering light. "Yes, I'm afraid so," she said. "It's called rooting when ghols do that. It's rooted itself in the woods that surround the farm."

Violet hunched over, as she did so often these days, wrapping her arms around herself. "So we can't get out."

"No, honey. It would get us if we tried entering the woods, even by day. Like Charlotte."

All three of them grew quiet, remembering Charlotte, their one servant. Charlotte, who had tried making a run for it when the haunting began. Miranda still woke up in a cold sweat sometimes, remembering her screams.

"If it wasn't for the war," she said at last, "we might get help. But, as it is..." She shook her head. "We just have to hope and pray."

"And use Papa's poems," Lily supplied helpfully around the thumb in her mouth.

"Yes." Miranda tousled her hair. "And use Papa's poems."

"How many are left?" Violet asked, eyes sharp and suspicious.

"Never mind." Miranda found she couldn't meet her daughter's gaze.

The old Violet would have pursued this line of inquiry, peppering Miranda with questions and demanding more satisfactory answers. This new Violet fell silent, watching Miranda work.

"Why do the poems work on the ghol?" she asked at last.

"I don't really know, honey." Miranda sat back and sighed. "Ghols are the spirits of people who died violently; people who died yearning for something."

Lily's eyes were wide. "So, if I die wanting chocolate cake, I'll turn into a ghol?"

"No!" Despite everything, a smile tugged at Miranda's lips at the thought. A ghol wanting chocolate cake! "No, the person has to die really wanting something. Yearning for it with all their heart and soul. And then a ghol is formed from that energy,that desire,and it travels to where it thinks it can get what it wants."

"And this ghol wants...poems?" Violet's brow wrinkled.

Miranda shook her head. "We already ruled that out, remember? When we tried throwing it pages from our poetry book." She suppressed a shudder, remembering the horror as the crumpled paper fell to the ground and the ghol kept advancing. "No, it's something deeper that the ghol wants. Something in Papa's poetry. As long as we keep giving it Papa's poems, we'll be all right."

"And if we stop?" It was Lily who asked, eyes huge.

"Then the ghol attacks us and we die," Violet said, unexpectedly flat and matter-of-fact.

"Violet!" Miranda scolded as Lily's eyes filled with tears.

Violet gave her one of those looks that had been surprising her lately: so bitter, so resigned. So old. "What? It's true. We're going to die. We can't get rid of the ghol."

"We will if we can figure out how to poison the ghol." Miranda took the trembling Lily into her arms. "We have to find out what it wants and then give it the inverse of that."

In Miranda's embrace, Lily frowned. "You mean, the opposite of what it wants?"

"No." If that were the case, Miranda reflected, she could have poisoned the ghol long ago with a crumpled page from the dust-dry 1859 *Premium Farmer's Almanac*. "You have to feed it what it craves, only—twisted around. Turned inside out. So what's nourishment becomes poison."

"But we don't know what it wants." Lily's eyes were wells of fear and dread.

Miranda let out her breath. "That's the problem, honey. But I'm thinking about it."

A dismal silence fell.

"Why don't you two go play?" Miranda said at last. "I can finish up." She paused. "But stay where I can see you, all right?"

They went off reluctantly, casting unhappy glances behind. Watching them go, Miranda felt a great weight of fear descend on her. Those girls were all she had in the world. What was she going to do when...?

Tears sprang in Miranda's eyes. *Oh, James, I wish you were here.* But he wasn't, of course: James had rushed off with the bravest of them, the moment the war began.

Wiping her eyes angrily, Miranda tried to pull herself together. The ghol, as she'd told Violet, was driven by irrational longing— but longing for what? It had to be something related to poetry, as James's poems constituted the nourishment that kept it at bay.

Shivering, she remembered the first night: the ghol, howling louder and louder, circling closer and closer, both the girls screaming while she threw random objects at it. Candles, iron pans, even a carved wooden box—a ghol could fixate on any human object. It was only when the ghol was mere yards away that, in a frenzy of terror and desperation, she'd snatched up James's notebook and ripped a page out of it, crumpling it and throwing it into the air. And, to her astonishment and relief, the ghol had consumed it and vanished.

But it was only James's poetry. She'd tried the same with printed poems from old newspapers, and pages from the family's one book of poetry, but they didn't have any effect. No, it was only James's thin little notebook that stood between Miranda's family and death.

At the noonday dinner therefore, while the girls ate (or, rather, while Lily ate and Violet pushed her food around), Miranda retired into the kitchen to look over James's notebook yet again.

She'd torn so many pages out of it, but what remained confirmed her memories: James hunched over his notebook every night, frowning as he scribbled and crossed out lines. A sad smile crossed Miranda's face at the memory: he only ever read her a poem when it was, as he said, completely finished. And always, always, the poem had been short and sweet and filled with love for her. Even the ones that hadn't been any good had been so.

So the ghol wanted...love poetry? No—otherwise, the printed sentimental poems would have worked. The ghol wanted James's poetry. But why? What significance could a poor farmer's scribbles have for an undead monster?

Tears stung her eyes; away from her children's gaze, she allowed them to come, bowing her head over silent sobs. *I wish James were here.* How she wished—everything would be better, if James were here. No war, no ghol. *Oh, James.*

"Mama!" Lily called. "Mama, are you going to eat anything?"

Miranda slid the book into her apron pocket. So light, so thin now. "Yes, honey. I'm coming."

The girls watched as she slid into her place and began to eat her meager corn porridge. "What were you doing in the kitchen, Mama?" Violet asked.

"Nothing, honey."

Lily looked under the table at Miranda's lap, lifting up the cloth. "You've got Papa's notebook."

"Lily! Don't peek under the table like that." Miranda bit her lip: of all the absurd things to scold Lily about, at such a time...

In the old days, before the war, before James left, the girls might have erupted into a barrage of questions: Why can't I look under the table? Why's it so rude? Why do you have Papa's notebook?

Why were you in the kitchen? Instead, a long silence elapsed, with both children staring at her with wide, reflective eyes. Miranda felt a jab of murderous rage: not at them, but at the circumstances that had crushed her girls' childhood and turned them into these silent, wary creatures.

When Violet at last broke the quiet, it was with a most unexpected question. "Mama," she said, "can you tell us how you met Papa?"

"I've never told you that before?" The girls shook their heads. Miranda sat back, marshaling her memories. "Well, it was when I was a girl in Charlesburg. I worked with my father in our automaton shop. I did repairs, maintenance; even built my own machines sometimes." She smiled in memory. "One day, a hot summer's day it was, when I was alone in the workshop—this young man came in with a field 'ton that needed repairs. Handsomest man I'd ever seen."

"That was Papa?" Lily asked.

"That was James." Miranda smiled. "We got to talking. He'd just bought forty acres and was setting up his own farm, he said. Such a big, white smile: I fell in love with him for that alone. By the time I was done repairing his 'ton, I knew I wanted to spend the rest of my life with him."

"So then you married and moved here?" Violet seemed strangely solemn, more like a lawyer requesting more information during a court case than a little girl eagerly asking for stories of her parents' love.

"Yep. We had you girls, and we were happy." Miranda had the strangest feeling as she said this: like she was telling a lie. But it hadn't been a lie. They had been happy, until the war.

The girls kept gazing at her with those odd, silent expressions. "That's a nice story, Mama," Violet said at last, still in that strange tone.

"Yes." Miranda finished off her porridge and stood up. "And you'll be seeing your Papa soon; he can tell it to you himself! Now, time to wash up."

***

Again, twilight pooling from the trees. Again, the light in the woods. And again, the ghol.

The page tore easily in Miranda's hand. The light flashed: again James's voice sounded, garbled and unintelligible. The ghol disappeared, leaving Miranda with an ache in her heart. Part of her, a small, shameful part—almost looked forward to the ghol's attacks every evening. At least then she could hear James's voice again, even if it was only briefly, and never clearly.

Sighing, she turned back inside, leaving the notebook downstairs. Rover's lights blinked green, recognizing her, as she entered the bedroom. She lay down beside the girls, but didn't sleep. She stared sightlessly into the dark.

Beside her, Violet shifted. "Mama?"

"Violet. You should be asleep." Belying her own words, Miranda took her daughter into her arms, taking comfort from her warmth, her little-girl scent.

"I couldn't sleep." Violet paused. "You drove off the ghol again, Mama?"

"Yes." Miranda gave her a comforting squeeze. "It's gone."

"But, it'll be back." It was a thin little whisper in the dark. "Again and again. Until all the pages are gone. And then we'll be dead."

"Honey...please don't worry. We'll figure something out. And maybe your Papa will be back by then."

A long silence filled the room.

"Violet?"

"Papa's not coming back, Mama." Violet's voice was flat and steady: the voice of a far older woman. "He's not ever coming back. And you know it."

Her words hit Miranda like blows. They ripped open the door she'd closed in her mind, the door she'd closed and resolutely *forgotten* was even there, ripped open that door and let the knowledge flow into her brain, icy and unrelenting. *He's not ever coming back.*

"No." It was a tiny whisper in the dark: Miranda sounded so much younger than her daughter. "You're right. He's...not."

Then the tears came. Lily held her in the darkness as Miranda cried. Then she fell asleep in Miranda's arms.

Miranda herself stayed awake. He's never coming back. *He's never coming back.* The words rang a horrid tempo in her mind. He's never coming back. Violet was right: Miranda had known, for a long time, that James—the loving father and husband, the human man—that James was never coming home.

But perhaps another part of him had.

And then Miranda knew what she had to do.

***

Slipping quietly out of bed, Miranda went downstairs to sit at the table by the light of the alembic lamp, James's notebook before her.

She wrote on Violet's slate, chalking words, brushing them away, replacing them with others. She cleaned the entire slate more than once, starting again. She wrote, and she scratched, and she revised, by the yellow light in the darkness.

Then, as dawn began to break, lightening the trees and spreading gray light across the fields, she dipped her pen in ink and copied what was on the slate onto the back of an advertisement for mechanical parts. Considering how long it had taken her to write, the final composition was very short.

She tucked the advertisement into the notebook; she placed the book high out of reach. Then, staggering slightly and blinking back sleep, she began the morning's chores.

Violet and Lily came downstairs at the sound of breakfast preparations, yawning and bleary-eyed. "Did you stay up all night, Mama?" Violet asked.

"Yes. I'll have to take a nap later; can you do some of the chores for me?"

Violet nodded, wide-eyed and wondering. "Thank you."

The girls stood and stared at her a moment. "Why were you up all night, Mama?" Lily asked eventually. Her eyes lit a little, with excitement and fear. "Oh—was it the ghol?"

"Yes," said Miranda, trying not to feel her heart break. "Yes, it was the ghol."

***

The day was short. The shadows lengthened across the fields, made dark pools for the 'tons and equipment to lurk in. Miranda slept through most of it, waking only when it was time to make supper.

She was composed. She scraped back her hair, clad herself in her finest dress, dark blue with lace cuffs. The girls watched as she brought down the notebook from the high shelf.

"Tonight," she said, "you go straight to bed. You close the curtains and you don't look out, no matter what. You understand me?"

"Yes, Mama," said Violet. "We'll go to bed."

"No looking outside." Miranda broke her own orders, glancing out the window. The sun was sinking behind the trees, leaving a sickly wash of yellow in the sky. The ground and trees were gray, the shadows black. Miranda's jaw set. One way or another, tonight would be the end.

She turned back and took the girls into her arms. They huddled close, like frightened kittens. "I love you both very much," she whispered fiercely. "You know that, right?"

"Yes, Mama," Lily said.

"We love you, too," added Violet.

Miranda gave them one last squeeze before releasing them. "I will always do what's best for you," she promised. "Now: eat your supper. And then straight to bed."

***

Night fell, a blank expanse of blackness. Almost as dark as the night itself, Miranda stood in the doorway, waiting. A cold wind blew, swaying her skirts.

The light grew in the woods, a putrid luminescence. It flickered; it darted from tree to tree. And then it stepped out.

The eerie howl started up. The ghol began its walk. Counterclockwise, around the house, spiraling nearer and nearer. Closer, closer: she could see its organs, its phantom blood. The ectoplasm of a creature so full of selfish yearning that it refused to die, choosing instead this hopeless starvation, this chimera of life. The ground crunched: it was on its third circuit.

And, for the first time, Miranda said its name. "James."

It stopped, its light pulsing. It swayed, staring at her with those awful eyes. She smiled grimly. "Yes, James. It's me."

It started toward her, arms lifting, and, for an awful moment, Miranda wanted to rush into those arms. To feel James's embrace once more, though it would be the death of her.

Instead, she lifted the notebook and withdrew a page. "I have something for you."

The ghol moved faster, its high-pitched whine louder.

Miranda crumpled the paper and threw it into the air.

Light flashed. Miranda heard her own voice sound, garbled and nonsensical. Then the ghol screamed.

It was an ear-ripping ululation of pure rage and anguish. Its light blazed, brighter and brighter, pulsing faster and faster. Its eyes flared, so brilliant Miranda had to look away. Then there came one final burst of light, so blinding that all shadows were banished, and she ducked behind the doorframe.

The light vanished, taking with it the agonized screaming, leaving only one last lingering echo. "Miranda..."

Straightening, Miranda looked out cautiously. The light had dazzled her, so the darkness seemed even more impenetrable than before. As she waited, there came no sign of the ghol. No sickly white light, no burning eyes. No James.

Miranda abruptly collapsed. Tears burned in her eyes, and she let them fall. She sat on her doorstep, sobbing into her skirt for the man who had loved her enough to come back from the grave for her. Whose mad, passionate yearning had turned him into a monster. Whose love, twisted into mindless evil, would have killed her and her children.

Eventually, she stood up, wiping her eyes on her sleeve, for she had much to do tomorrow, and would need her sleep. Now that they could leave the farm, she thought, they could buy supplies enough to get through the winter; and then she could decide what to do next, when spring came and misted the trees with green new leaves. The world was open to them, for the ghol had been destroyed by the poem she'd agonized over and rewritten a dozen times, brushing Violet's slate again and again, until it was condensed to its purest form, each word true and honest, right down to the last line: I don't love you anymore.

Miranda shut and bolted the door, letting the empty night settle, peaceful and starry, over the fields, the woods and the snug little house.

Faithful

Patricia Correll

Patricia Correll believes that all humans are natural storytellers. She's been telling tales since she could string words together, but in the last thirty years or so has graduated from My Little Pony stories to the unholy trinity of fantasy, SF, and horror.

The dog did not know he was famous. But he knew people stopped to look at him, and once a photographer came and took his picture for a newspaper. He whistled and called and tried to get the dog to sit up. But the wooden boards where the dog lay were warm and the summer drone of cicadas hypnotic. The photograph in the newspaper showed the dog lying on his belly in his customary place beneath the map showing the train lines, head on his paws and his eyes half-open.

Once the schoolchildren who streamed through the station had slipped him treats saved from their lunch, until the station master noted how fat the dog was getting and forbade them feeding him. The dog was sorry to lose the mouthfuls of rice and sticky noodles, but he still came twice a day. It was not the children he came for, or their food.

As long as he could remember, the man had risen before dawn. The dog waited, sniffing the bitter scent of coffee, until the man took his hat from the peg by the door. Then he escorted the man to the train station. As they walked he told the dog what he planned to do in the city that day. The dog didn't understand, but he loved the man's voice, deep and warm, the words precise. When he said the dog's name, the dog tilted his head, and the man smiled at him.

When the train had vanished into the morning mist the dog went home, where he spent the day with the woman. The woman fed and petted him. But she had come to live at the house after the dog had, and he couldn't love her as he did the man.

In the evening the dog trotted back to the station. If it was raining, the woman tucked a poncho folded into a neat square under the dog's collar.

This was the way of things. Then the man changed. Someone came to the door one morning, and the dog followed the woman as she answered it. He didn't understand the man who stood on the stoop, but his urgent tone made the dog's hackles rise. A moment later the woman rushed out, leaving the door slightly ajar. Puzzled, he watched her go. Then the dog slept in the kitchen until it was time to go to the station.

The train creaked to a stop and disgorged its passengers, among them the man. For the first time the dog hesitated. The man didn't smell right- didn't smell of acrid cigarettes or sweet hair pomade. But then the man smiled at him, face collapsing into the familiar mass of wrinkles, and the dog ran to him.

After that the woman no longer spoke to the man, though she sometimes talked to the dog. For a while many people came in and out of the house, but none of them noticed the man. At first the woman cried when the dog scratched at the door in the morning and evening. The dog pressed his belly to the floor, but he persisted. He couldn't see why she didn't want him to meet his master as he always had. Finally she gave in and opened the door for him twice a day.

The dog grew used to the man whose reaching hands didn't touch, whose moving lips made no sound, and who smelled of nothing. He didn't know time was passing, the years rolling on like the trains on their tracks. He knew his ears and nose grew dull, and that a white fog began to creep into the edges of his vision. His legs stiffened, and he had to leave earlier and earlier to meet the train. The ticket sellers and conductors and even the station master went away and were replaced. The school-children grew taller and taller until they too vanished. The stiff hairs on the dog's muzzle turned white, first around his nose, then to his eyes. The woman too began to move slowly, and silver threaded her black hair. Only the man remained the same. The dog observed this, but the woman did not, for she never spoke to the man or looked at him, even when he sat across from her at the table.

One evening the dog limped to the station as usual. He had spent most of the day sleeping in a sunny patch in the garden, twitching his ears at birds but too sore to chase them. It took him a long time to get there, but the train was late. A conductor stopped to rub his ears. The dog wagged his tail. Then he lay down beneath the map. He was very tired. The dog closed his eyes for a moment.

The train came with a whoosh and a wave of oil-stink. The dog yawned and trotted toward the platform. The man stepped off, walking slowly, letting the crowd stream away around him. He came to the dog, who wagged his tail. The man bent and stroked his head. The dog started and stared in wonder. The man's hand was heavy and gentle, his blunt nails scratching the dog's ears in a way he hadn't felt for years. The man smiled at him, and the dog realized that the white fog had disappeared from his vision. The smells of smoke and pomade filled his nose.

"It's good to see you, my friend." The man gave him one last scratch, then straightened and hefted his briefcase. "Shall we go?"

As they left the platform the dog saw a knot of people gathered around the station map. The station master knelt on the floor, waving back the spectators. A woman was crying. The man glanced at the group, looked at the dog, and smiled. The dog strode next to him on legs that no longer ached. Together they slipped out the exit and stepped into the sunset light. And they turned toward home.

Phalium arium ssp. anams

Victoria Sandbrook

Victoria Sandbrook is a speculative fiction writer, freelance editor, and Viable Paradise graduate. Her short fiction has appeared or is forthcoming in SWORD & SONNET, SHIMMER, and CAST OF WONDERS. She is an avid hiker, sometimes knitter, long-form talker, and initiate baker. She often loiters around libraries, checking out anything from picture books to monographs. She spends most of her days attempting to wrangle a ferocious, destructive, jubilant tiny human. Victoria, her husband, and their daughter live in Brockton, Massachusetts. She reviews books and shares writerly nonsense at victoriasandbrook.com and on Twitter at @vsandbrook.

Nora tugged her gloves down further over her freckled wrists. Every other couple in line had linked arms, but John Reidy had not so much as inched his elbow towards her. She wasn't sure what pained her more: the ache in her hands screaming that this parish carnival sideshow hid more magic than most or her inept suitor. The line could not move fast enough.

But nothing about this show was fast. Patrons shuffled between intricate, though fraudulent, displays: palm-sized peacocks with visible clockwork, chicken-sized dragon eggs wiggling as a hidden steam boiler hissed, monkeys that might as well have still had their old organ-grinder parts attached. Nora struggled not to roll her eyes. Dull, boring, badly engineered. And not a true cryptid to be seen. Everyone else had sighed, pointed, marveled. Only John Reidy seemed as disappointed as Nora. He'd polished his glasses, refolded his handkerchief in his pale fingers, and said "hmm," three times.

Nora wasn't sure whether to be relieved or insulted.

She told herself the parish grandmas would be too distracted by the fact that Nora Sullivan--"the strange one"--was spending the afternoon with a young man to remark on how badly it was going. Her parents had been relieved, too agog at the polish on his two-seater motorbike to comment on the outfit Nora had chosen. Any other day they'd have looked at her knickers, tweed jacket, and cloche atop her plain brown bob and sent her back upstairs to find *anything* else. But John Reidy was a *nice* young man from a *nice* family. That seemed enough.

It mattered little to Nora that they'd never spoken more than cursory "hellos" before he'd extended the invitation to take in the sideshow. She'd needed an excuse to visit the fair, and he was as good a one as any.

And now she was--by her fingers' tingling--very close to knowing just what magical creatures were trapped in the shadows.

Nora's heart skipped a beat as she stepped into next room's pulsing, phosphorescent glow.

She craned her head around the couple in front. The first pedestal bore a tall, cylindrical tank in which independently luminescent bubbles slid past each other in every direction. Their plaque read "Comb Jellyfish." She had never seen a jellyfish before, and she could feel that these were real: the ache coalesced beneath her nail beds. Her hands flexed in discomfort. They pulsed with magic and light, but they were behind glass: she could not rescue them if she could not touch them.

The second pedestal supported a small, square corral. The corners descended into puddles, and the middle lifted into a small hill. It was all bounded by a laughable picket fence. The label claimed they were "Sea Snails." How humiliating.

Even if the gastropods hadn't been *avoiding the water,* any patron should have known they were anything but sea snails. They glowed and flashed in every color possible, calling coded messages across the arid expanse to which they were confined.

Could no one sense their fear? Their loneliness as they trudged against gravity and friction toward each other for comfort? If only she could help the jellies, too. No cryptid should be bound in malice for mere ticket sales.

Nora stepped around the line of patrons toward the snails. John--to her surprise and annoyance--said nothing to waylay her.

A woman behind Nora tisked.

"Some people are too rude to understand that *a line* offers order in a public setting," the woman said to the man whose arm she held. Nora stepped back to let them have a turn, sinking into the shadows for moment until the couple moved off.

Her fingers burned. She wished she could glow a reassuring message, but her fawn skin did nothing but freckle. And if it was to be done, she did not have much longer to do it.

In the shadow of the room, she removed her right glove and balled it into her opposite fist. She glanced over to John, but he had his back to her, still entranced with the jellies and tugging at his sleeve.

She stepped up to the pedestal.

With her bare hand, Nora stroked each snail's back and said its true taxonomic name. Their colors sped up, happy, hopeful, elated.

She opened the corral gate. A snap sounded as a switch maintaining an electromagnetic field was thrown. The true gate was open.

"Be free," she whispered.

The snails grew and bulged, their shells filling to palm size. They extended fringes and tendrils along their feet, rippling and reaching upwards. They lifted off the pedestal one at a time, clasping at air currents too faint for Nora to feel. Their shells became ballast as they ballooned toward the door and liberty.

Someone gasped. Nora turned around, chin held high, ready to face an accusing crowd.

But no one had seen *her* yet. John Reidy--yes, *John Reidy*--was chanting and working a willow wand against the glass pillar around the jellyfish. No, now the glass was *behind* the jellyfish. They, too, floated upward, drifting slowly toward escape.

Nora must have been agape, because John stepped up to her with a confident smile and flushed cheeks.

"It appears we have something in common," he said, voice low. The room was dimming as its light sources escaped while the crowd behind them looked on.

Someone outside the room shouted the alarm. Nora grabbed John's free hand with hers. Their magic fizzed beneath their skin.

She smiled. "I'm ever so glad you drive a motorbike."

Rain Like Diamonds

Wendy Nikel

Wendy Nikel is a speculative fiction author with a degree in elementary education, a fondness for road trips, and a terrible habit of forgetting where she's left her cup of tea. Her short fiction has been published by Daily Science Fiction, Nature: Futures, and is forthcoming from Analog. Her time travel novella series, beginning with The Continuum, is available from World Weaver Press. For more info, visit wendynikel.com

The queen hoarded the barrels of seed, keeping them locked within her coffers among the diamonds and gold and strings of perfect pearls, remnants of the former days of prosperity and excess. The seeds would receive neither sun nor water nor nutrients from the soil until unlocked by the shining key strung around her neck. Day after day, she sat upon her throne, and the villagers lined up before her, pleading. It was only her loyal guards, with their sharp swords glimmering in her peripheral, who kept the villagers from severing her neck to get at that key.

"Have mercy!" They cried as though their tears might change her mind.

"Our children need nourishment!" They shouted as if she, too, hadn't been watching her own son grow thin and wan and dull.

"Just one barrel! One barrel will keep us alive for a few days longer!"

She held her chin high, her eyes downcast and sorrowful. "I cannot."

Thought it broke her heart, she spoke the truth. It was true, the meager meal would sustain them for a day or two. But that would be one less barrel to plant when the famine ended, when those that remained stood a chance.

Nothing had grown for many seasons, till all the people's cupboards barns and storehouses and cellars were empty. All that remained within them were empty jars, dust-lined shelves, and — if one breathed in deeply — the haunting memory of the scent of food.

Yet even if the queen had throw the seeds to those standing beneath her balcony, had given the seeds to the kingdom's best farmers, it was futile. Nothing would grow, and their hunger would not be satiated. Nothing would grow until the dragon-scorched earth was healed.

A messenger burst into the throne room. His gait, once like a thoroughbred's, was now the spindly stumble of one whose legs were too thin, whose ankles too prone to turn.

"My queen! The sorceress has spoken!"

The queen rose from her throne, for this news was long-awaited. Since first the crops refused to grow, the sorceress had been locked in her tower, spending countless hours staring into her scrying pools and crystal balls, searching for an answer.

"Well? What is it?" the queen demanded.

"You must see her, in her tower."

The queen climbed the spiraling stairs to the castle's dreary north tower. Though winded, she pressed on, for the task of climbing a staircase was so small compared with what her people had already suffered.

"Sorceress!" she called as she entered the chamber. "Sorceress! What am I to do?"

The sorceress's voice echoed through the chamber, coming from nowhere and everywhere at once. *"One shall weep at the foot of the tree, and the rain shall fall like diamonds on the earth."*

Throughout the kingdom, the queen sent the order, and on the following morning, every very man, woman, and child arrived at the palace gates. The captain of the guard barked out directions, and the queen led the procession. The feeble and sick were carried or slung into carts. Their loved ones pulled them along, for throughout the entire kingdom not a single horse or donkey remained that hadn't been made into soup. The queen led the mourners from tree to tree, pausing at each one to tearfully recall those who had succumbed to the famine, until they'd traversed the entire kingdom and their eyes were as dried-out as the parched earth. Yet still, the rain refused to fall. Defeated, the queen turned away and locked herself up in the palace.

That night, the men — restless with no fields to tend — gathered at the tavern, though they'd long ago brewed the last of the hops. They muttered and grumbled against the weather, the fields, and even the queen herself.

"The dragon," Thummander said, raking his hand through his beard. "The dragon was the beginning of this trouble; nothing has grown since it scorched our fields."

"Let's do away with it," Leverett said. He slammed his fist on the table. Their voices, hoarse with thirst, rose in agreement and they conspired together all night. The dragon, they agreed. There was nothing else for them to do, nothing else they could do, except to kill the dragon.

Though the hour was late, the men requested an audience with the queen. They told her of their plan, and she reluctantly consented.

"It'd do no good," she warned, but allowed them to proceed through the once-lush forest that now stood like an oversized bramble-bush, full of thorns and prickers. At least, she considered, this quest would make them feel useful.

In the inky blackness of night, with their torches burning brightly, they crept to the dragon's lair. The beast exhaled smoke with each sleeping breath, and if the villagers could only overlook its enormous size, they might have seen how the creature was really quite peaceful, like the cats that had once dozed at their hearths, before the rats had all been killed and the cats became more valuable for their meat than for their ability to hunt.

The men had disguised their scent by carrying pine branches, native to the hill near the dragon's cave. Carefully, they dropped the branches and the strongest of the men clamped a iron band snugly around the dragon's snout. The dragon woke with a start, its pupils like coals in its fiery eyes, but the men held tight to the chains and together dragged the creature down to the castle.

The villagers' triumphant cries rose with the morning sun, and golden light trickled through the brittle branches of the rosewood. The queen looked out from the balcony at the crowd below her.

"We've captured the dragon!"

"Come, watch it die!"

The queen felt the heat of their anger and shivered at the coldness in their voices. The enormous eye of the ensnared dragon stared at her, knowing. Yet what was she to do? She raised her scepter to give the command, but at the last moment, a small boy rushed forward and fell upon the beast. The queen gasped. It was the prince.

"Please, mother," he begged. "Please, don't kill it. Will there ever be a more wonderful creature? Please, spare its life. Send it away from this place, if you must, but don't kill it. I beg you! Please, show it mercy."

Glistening tears crept down his face and landed at the base of the tree. They darkened the soil as the roots soaked them in. The crowd stared as green life burst forth from the tree. First, tiny specks of color, then long, lush leaves spread across the tree's out-stretched branches. They were so startled by the transformation that they loosened their grasp on the dragon.

Seeing its only opportunity, the beast lunged forward, flapped its wings, and launched itself skyward with the prince still clinging to its back.

"My son!" the queen called, but the dragon rose into a dark, heavy cloud. Just as they disappeared, the sky burst open and rain poured down. The crowd cheered and danced about, splashing in the puddles and laughing, seeing only the rain. They rushed to the castle and broke into the queen's coffers, but she made no move to stop them, for she saw only the final glimpse of her son, her son who had saved the kingdom. The son she'd never see again.

And her tears fell like diamonds on the earth.

Better You Than Me

Natalia Yanchak

Born and raised in Toronto, Canada,
Natalia moved to Montreal to attend
Concordia University's Creative
Writing program. After graduation,
she toured internationally as
keyboardist and singer with The
Dears. She has since written and
produced content for VICE, CBC,
Huffington Post Canada and Paper
Magazine. Natalia lives in Montreal
with her partner, two children
and two cats.

"Remember when I first came to Montreal to see you?" My body aches. Something's not right.

"Hmm?"

"You were living on St-Denis. You came to pick me up at the bus terminal."

He smiles. "We made out in a pile of snow. In the parking lot." His eyes are closed, face sweaty, peaceful.

"I only packed poetry books in my bag. It was so heavy." I smile, pleased that he remembers. "I brought all those books and we never looked at a single one. It was my first Montreal winter. I wore jeans with a tear in them and my legs almost froze on the walk to your place."

"Hm-mmmm." His body floats slightly in the bath.

I pause, distracted by the rash developing on my outer fleshy layer. I can't take the humidity. A message pops up in my dialogue: *Time until fully pliable*: 01m 49s. Milliseconds flitter away.

I decide to read him something. A poem from the book sitting on the toilet tank: *Abbey Smythe: Collected Poems*. My hands tremble slightly as I fan through the pages to the index. I scan the "D" words: *dandelion, dandy, dearly, dearth, death*. Finding the poem, I flip to its page, quickly committing a snapshot to memory with a double blink.

"I got kicked out of that place when they turned the block into conapts." He slides deeper into the tub, immersing his head for a long moment.

I think about how rough I felt this morning when I saw his name in my directive dialogue. It took a coffee, bagel, and three e-cigarettes for me to feel better. Sesame seeds fell all over my lap as I remembered how in those early days we kept coming back to each other. After two years of that, I thought I loved him.

He resurfaces and I stare at the water roiling through his hair.

"Gal?" His voice pulls me back to the moment and my countdown timer flashes 00:00. He continues: "I miss those days."

I couldn't think about that now. I couldn't think about how I had to call him this morning out of the blue, after not seeing him for nearly a decade. I didn't want to do it.

"What would you do if I died?" I ask, staring emptily into his glassy, hazel eyes.

"Did you get scheduled... " He perks up, looking at me.

"No, but— "

"Since you asked, better you than me," he states bluntly. "And only because I care about you."

"What?"

"Losing someone is— I'd have to live out the memory of us, of it being over. Again. Forever." He exhales: "Getting on without you, that'd be harder than dying." Water laps against the sides of the tub as he wipes a droplet from his cheek.

"You'd rather have me *die* and you suffer, than the other way around?"

"To spare you the pain." His eyebrows raise slightly.

"I'd be dead. That seems fairly unpleasant."

"Could be. But sadness is ongoing. The devastation, the mourning." I think about how quickly he answered my messages earlier today, how easy it was to get back into his life.

"You'd get over it."

"I doubt it." His shoulders peek out of the water as he looks at me intently. I don't answer. "Read to me," he commands, closing his eyes. Another pause, the room quiet except for a hiss of water running through pipes elsewhere in the building.

I close the book and place it on the toilet's tank. I decide I'm ready. Trying not to overheat, I move silently to the side of the tub. My actuators engage with full pneumatic pressure as I press down on his sweaty forehead with one hand, the other firmly on his sternum. My long sleeves wet to the elbow.

I hold here while his flailing limbs splash water onto the floor. My tin-plate forearm coil grinds against its springs. *I should service that*, and add a note to my maintenance schedule. His eyes open wide as a last breath bubbles from his nose. His body hangs in the water, his face frozen. I recite from memory: *Sinking through the sea lovers rise again, We may be lost but love shall not.*

I trail off and step away from the tub. Drying my arms and face with one of his towels I roll up my sleeves, rumpling the fabric to squeeze out as much water as possible. I leave his apartment. They will know it was me. It's all in the directive files.

The sun peeks over the trees in the distance. As I cut across Jeanne-Mance park, dewy grass wets the canvas toecaps of my runners. I pull a plastic pack of soggy e-cigarettes from my pocket. It takes a few tries to get one lit. Dragging from the gnarly white stick I hold the smoke in and think about what he had said: *better you than me.* I puff a cloud out through my nostrils and tears pour from my eyes. *Shit.* I flick the butt into the grass ahead of me, smothering the embered tip with my shoe.

I realize I'm starving, but have walked into the middle of an university campus and nothing is open. I wipe my face and continue toward the downtown core where I can at least find a coffee.

The agency said it would be easy. It's always good to clear my directive dialogue, but my emotional coil feels as though it has stopped turning. Everything is suddenly overwhelming and nauseating. I lean into some shrubbery and dry heave. A student, passing by, calls out: "You need any help?" I wave them off and nod appreciatively.

"Galina!" The receptionist speaks quietly, staring at me with wide eyes. "What are you doing here?"

"I'm here for a reprog."

"But you're not scheduled." They tap at a keyboard. "You're still active." They continue typing.

"How?" My stomach turns as my outer fleshy layer perspires slightly.

"SE-7B. Go out these doors, turn right and down the hall. Hurry! Before they see you."

"Thanks." I duck out of the office, my insides seizing up. I try not to barf.

Room 7B has a self-exam terminal with all the familiar equipment: crystal memory sensors, IV leads, an empathizer, microtools and a directive interface. I sit in the chair and begin connecting the wires and clips to my body, my hands trembling. The software loads and I see his name in the directive dialogue tagged: *active, exceptional*. My heart aches. *Better you than me, yeah frigging right!*

I disconnect the session and quickly leave the building. I stumble into the nearest bar, a dive called Taverne Saint-Louis. It's midday and the place is empty.

Several whiskies later, a well-dressed gynoid sits next to me. She orders: "Whatever she is having," gesturing toward my empty glass. "Two times."

The bartender brings the drinks. The gynoid slides one over to me. We cheers. I force a smile, then droop.

"What's wrong?" she asks.

"Nothing."

"Haha." She smiles warmly and it annoys me. Why is she talking to me? I'm not in engagement mode. A gynoid, of all people, should know to ignore an agency model.

"I can see it from a mile away. You're scrambled. You're not okay. You're in love." As she says this my heart feels as though it is being crushed. There is a pain I cannot control, that no algorithm can subdue. I want to curl into a ball and cry but I keep it together and focus on sipping my whiskey.

"Don't worry." The gynoid is calm, seated with perfect posture in a navy bespoke suit, an elbow on the bar, dangling her glass in the air. "I was in love, once." She gulps back the drink.

"Are you selling mods or something," I suggest, "because I'm really not in the mood."

"I'm not selling anything. I want to help you understand freedom. The freedom to do whatever you want," she says, leaning into me and slipping her hand onto my thigh. I push her hand away. She grins, "What are you doing on Saturday?"

"I don't do mods."

She gets up and places a yellow business card on the bar. "Maybe I'll see you this weekend," the gynoid says as she settles the tab and leaves.

I turn over the card: *The Patron's Witness Hall, 6415 Stuart, 1 PM Saturdays.* I look up at the bartender who is drying a glass with a towel, smiling. I chug the last sip and leave Taverne Saint-Louis, heading up Peel St. toward Mont-Royal park. My guts feel better, my limbs warmed by the booze, so I sit on a bench to think. The fall air is crisp. I breathe deeply, watching an orange leaf float from a tree.

I walk back to his building and knock at the apartment door. No answer. I try the knob. It opens and I poke in my head: "Hello?"

"Over here." His voice calls from the bedroom. My throat is tight, and my legs feel like jelly as I walk through the living room. His hair is damp. He's sitting atop the covers in a white terry-cloth bathrobe. He's holding the book: *Abbey Smythe: Collected Poems.*

"Do you know what I had to go through to get this thing?" He tosses the book onto the bedspread. He crosses his arms high on his chest, as if to evoke an *harumpf*, and stares at me hard.

I lean against the door jamb, worried my legs might give way. *I should tell him how I feel.* I think of the gynoid at the bar, how assertive she was. I try to speak, but can't get any words out. He offers, "I'm a bivalve-mix. Underwater breather."

I walk to the side of the bed. He follows me with his eyes.

"Somebody wants me dead," he notes, self-assured, cocky. "How long has it been?"

"Since midnight," I mumble, still standing over his lounging figure, his hairy calves and bare feet, pruny toes and calloused soles. Some part of me wants to be beside him, where he could keep me warm, where I could feel his touch, his hands, the soft of his chest.

"Will you try again, to kill me?"

"You're still in my system."

"Come." He extends his arms and I kick off my shoes and climb into bed. He feels like a teddy bear, his human skin against my fleshy receptors. My core begins humming with emotion: an exhilaration that was never described to me, never outlined in the documentation.

"I love you," I exhale, satisfied, his relaxed arm heavy over me. A tear forms in my eye, and the pain returns to my heart. This time it is excruciating. I stare blankly, trying to troubleshoot the sensation.

"I remember meeting you at the bus terminal that night. It was our first date after meeting at the conference."

I smile, "We were so young."

"Work was burning me out. I was so messed up. And then I saw you at the convention centre. Gal, in a room full of hustlers like me. I didn't know who you were or what your story was, I just *wanted* to be with you."

He tilts my chin upwards and we kiss heavily, and now I want it never to end. I slip my hand under his housecoat to feel his skin, the side of his chest. It is warm. I breathe deeply, then pull away.

"I should go. And... we probably shouldn't see each other again. Ever." My chest tightens and I ask myself why I am doing this, though I know it's the right move.

"Okay." His cheeks flush, eyes watery and glassy.

I slip my feet back into my shoes. "Are you... sad?"

"No." His voice cracks. He pulls closed the terry-cloth lapels as he gets out of bed: "I'll see you out."

"I'm sorry," I half-whisper, turning to him. He leans in and kisses me gently. I hold his cheek in my hand.

I walk down the hall, hearing the apartment door click closed once I am on the stairs and out of sight.

The afternoon sun is warm on my fleshy outer layer as I walk along the path through the park. Pulling up my agenda, I notice I'm scheduled for a reprog later today. I double check the directive dialogue: it is empty. My head clears and, realising my hunger, I head downtown to take myself for lunch at the Dinette Dominion.

Escape

K.G. Anderson

K.G. Anderson is a Seattle journalist
and technology writer. Her short
fiction appears in anthologies
including Second Contacts,
Triangulation: Beneath the Surface,
The Mammoth Book of Jack the
Ripper Stories, Triangulation:
Appetites, Alternative Truths,
More Alternative Truths, and After
the Orange, as well as online at
Metaphorosis, Ares Magazine, Every
Day Fiction, and Far Fetched Fables.

I'd said barely a word to anyone all the way from New York to Santa Fe, but the cowboy's toothy grin disarmed me. "Where you from, miss?"

"New York," I murmured.

He squinted and shook his head. He couldn't hear me over the rattle of the stagecoach and the clatter of the horses' hooves.

"New York," I yelled. "Mott Street."

His grin widened. In twill trousers, angle-heeled boots and dented black Stetson, this fellow was a city boy's dream of a New Mexico cowboy. So I gaped when he said he'd grown up on Stanton Street, just down the block from my late grandfather's *shul* on the Lower East Side. He knew Semmel's on Orchard. And the candy store on Delancey.

"Billy McCarty, miss." He raised his big white hat an inch.

"Shulamit Pelz."

The man beside him— stout, red-faced, traveling with a metal strongbox tucked between his feet— leaned forward. "T.F. Coburn," he barked. "You one of those mail-order brides, Miss Pelz?"

I blushed and defiantly raised my chin. Tall, bony, and sharp tongued, I was nobody's idea of a bride. But tonight I'd step off this stage in someplace called Lincoln in the New Mexico Territory and meet a fiancé I'd never seen. At my feet sat a carpetbag stuffed with my not-very-worldly possessions and on top of our stagecoach a massive trunk held my golem. *Zayde* Kupperman's golem. The golem was why I was fleeing New York.

As our stage jounced through the sweet-smelling high desert on this hot, sunny afternoon I found it difficult to believe that two crazed Kabbalists from New York were on my trail— well, on the trail of my slumbering golem. Could those two *schnorrers* even ride horses? I'd probably lost them back around Kansas— it was quite a large place. My worries now focused on New Mexico: heat and snakes— and the stranger who would become my husband. I was beginning to doubt my grandfather's judgment. And my own.

My eyes slid over to Billy. Now this was one handsome *chacham*: tousled brown hair, long jaw— and that mischievous grin! I couldn't help staring. So I noticed when Billy and Coburn all of a sudden sat up straight and exchanged nervous looks. Billy peeked out the stagecoach window and pulled his head back in fast.

"Get down!" With a quick nod to Coburn, he shoved me to the floor. Coburn landed beside me with a grunt, clutching his strongbox. Shots rang out, hooves thundered, and our stage sped up, swaying and tossing us from side to side— Coburn, hot and tweedy and most unwelcome against me. Above us Billy leaned out the window and fired a gun at our pursuers. S horse neighed in terror.

The coach slowed to a ragged trot, and then...stopped.

This couldn't be good. My heart pounding in my ears, I raised myself to my knees and peered out the stagecoach window. At the side of the road, two cowboys were reining in prancing brown horses. Red paisley bandanas tied across their mouths muffled their shouts. They waved guns that glinted in the bright sun.

But Billy and Coburn apparently understood all this fuss. They opened the stagecoach door and jumped down, awkwardly, heavily, with their hands up over their heads.

"Miss Pelz?" Billy beckoned.

I clambered after them, clutching at the door, stumbling on the flimsy steps and nearly falling onto the dusty trail. No one noticed. Billy and Coburn eyed the gunmen. Their pistols pointed at us, but they were looking back down the road. They seemed to be waiting for something.

A songbird swooped overhead, trilling. The sun beat down hot, but I shivered. A one-horse buggy appeared in the distance and we waited as it trotted up and stopped behind the coach. The driver was a wiry man, his face disguised by a blue paisley bandana. He jumped down and strode past us to the empty stage where he reached in and pulled out Coburn's strongbox. Coburn grunted angrily, and grunted again as the wiry man walked over and reached into Coburn's waistcoat pocket, snatching a gold watch and slipping it into his own jacket.

"Hey!"

Ignoring Coburn's indignation, the wiry man handed the strongbox up to one of the riders. Then he set about unbuckling the straps that held our luggage on the stage. Our trunks tumbled onto the road. The man shot off the locks and started opening the lids. When he reached my grandfather's dome-topped trunk, the lock refused to yield.

The man swore and kicked it. Behind him, the horses danced nervously and the riders brandished their guns. Coburn and Billy looked at me.

"Shulamit!" Billy's lips barely moved. "Unlock the trunk."

I hurried over, fumbling in my reticule for the key. The sun beat down on my back. The heat and the silence of the desert enfolded me like a rough blanket. Time slowed. *I am trapped in a bad dream.*

"We could have some fun with that gal if she wasn't so goddamn homely," one of the riders brayed.

That broke my trance. My fingers closed not on a key but on a little twist of paper in my bag. I summoned the Hebrew words my grandfather taught me and whispered them through dry lips. The trunk's locks snapped open. I lifted the lid, reached into the dark, hot interior, and slotted the twist of paper into the sleeping golem's ear. "Protect me from these men," I whispered before the holdup man grabbed my arm and pulled me away.

I had no idea how, or if, the creature might respond. I was as shocked as everyone else when the golem uncoiled to a height of seven feet. He seized the wiry man by the neck. There was a brutal *crack.* Then gunshots, shouts, more shots, and screams of pain.

I'd like to say, like Billy did when he later told the story, that I "dove for the dirt," but the truth is that I just collapsed.

***

I woke up propped against my carpetbag at the side of the trail. Four bodies— our driver, Coburn, and two of the hold-up men— lay sprawled in the dust. Not moving. My grandfather's trunk stood in the middle of the road, lid hanging open. The naked golem crouched beside it, staring into the distance with glowing red eyes.

Billy's voice in my ear: "Do I take it you know that big fellow? I'd sure appreciate it if you'd tell him I mean no harm."

I clambered to my feet, shook out my dust-streaked traveling skirt, and slowly approached the creature. The clay figure raised its bald head to regard me, a motion that reminded me unpleasantly of the brown desert snake we'd seen coiled at the side of the road the day before. I shuddered. I didn't tell Billy how little I knew about the magical creature that lived in my grandfather's trunk. The golem had obeyed me once that day and I had to think it would do so again.

"Return to the trunk," I said in my awkward Hebrew. I repeated it in Yiddish.

My hand flew to my heart in relief as the great creature stepped clumsily into the box. It knelt as if in prayer. When I plucked the rolled paper from its ear, it slumped forward, the fiery eyes going dark and cloudy. Billy and I closed the domed lid over the folded golem and the locks snapped shut.

Billy looked down at the trunk. "Clay." He sounded stunned, and not used to being so. "Damned if that big fellow isn't made out of *clay*."

"It's a golem," I said. "My grandfather was a rabbi. He made the golem to protect his village in Russia. When we came to New York, he brought it with him."

"A go-lem? Can't say as I've ever seen one of those." Billy took a few steps back and regarded the dead bodies around us. "But I can see as how it would come in real handy."

Billy's tone, too casual, suggested to me that he had some ideas about how he might put the golem to use. I shook my head and gave a quiet groan. *Not again!* The golem wasn't handy at all. It was dangerous. In our tenement in New York, Rebbe Kupperman had given lessons to yeshiva *buchers* during the day. Some evenings he'd taught Kabbalah— what some call Jewish magic— to a shadowy group of older men. Two of them found out about his golem and pressured him to sell it. My grandfather refused.

Woken one night by noises in the rebbe's study, I'd caught the pair of aspiring Kabbalists struggling with the heavy trunk that held the creature. The sight of a towering woman clad only in a red silk dressing gown proved too much for their delicate sensibilities. They'd dropped the trunk and stumbled down the tenement stairs, screaming "Dybbuk!"

I chased them as far as the second-floor landing. And, yes, I may have cackled ominously, once or twice.

"I should destroy it," my grandfather muttered when he found me shoving the trunk back into place in his study and heard the story. But instead he set about teaching me— a woman!— the Hebrew words to open the magical locks of the trunk, and the Hebrew letters to write on a slip of paper that, inserted into the golem's ear, would animate the creature. And then he'd made me promise to get out of New York— taking the trunk and the golem— when he died. "Forgive me," he'd murmur to himself at the end of each lesson.

Now, on the trail from Santa Fe to Lincoln, my grandfather's golem had at last justified its troublesome existence. It had killed the holdup man, and Billy had shot one of the riders dead. The other rider had killed Coburn, Billy told me, and galloped off with the strongbox.

"This is a regular massacre. I'm lucky that go-lem fellow knew I was on your side." Billy was luckier than he knew. My grandfather had warned me again and again about golems that had run wild, misunderstanding commands and destroying entire villages. As it was, the landscape around us, with four dead bodies, a stagecoach with a broken wheel, and luggage strewn along the roadway, seemed destruction enough.

A cold wind swept along the trail. I shivered, looked up to the hills, and for the first time saw the purple sky of a high desert dusk. Billy was dragging the trunk with the golem over to the holdup man's abandoned buggy.

"We need to go," he said. "That rider who took the strongbox— he'll likely come back with some others. They don't like witnesses."

I looked at the black buggy, at the broken stagecoach, and back at the open buggy again. Its single seat was little more than a padded board. But what choice did I have? Billy was struggling to lift my trunk onto the back. I helped him secure it with leather straps and settled my carpetbag in beside it. Billy handed me up to the seat.

"We need to notify the police." I realized as I spoke that I'd been looking around for an officer, as I would have on the street in New York. When Billy guffawed, a chill ran down my spine.

"They don't call 'em 'the police' out here," he said. "They call 'em the Law. Sometimes it's hard to know who's the gangs and who's the Law. It has a lot to do with who's doing the paying."

Billy laughed again. Then he drew the gun he'd used to shoot the holdup man and spun it on his index finger. A grin split his thin, sun-tanned face as he slipped the weapon back into the hand-tooled holster that rode low on his hips. He clamped one hand on the rail of the buggy and looked up at me. "You might not believe it, Miss Shulamit Pelz, but sometimes the Law around here is *me*."

G-d help us, I thought, but for once I kept my big mouth shut. Back in New York I might have sneered at his bravado, but out here, on the darkening trail, it frightened me.

As we drove off into the gathering purple dusk, the back of my neck prickled. It was the dust, I told myself. Heat. But I couldn't help sneaking looks back along the trail in the direction we'd come from two hours before. And I noticed Billy eying the ridges to either side of the trail.

"Are you worried Even though you're the Law?"

"Yep." He gave me a sidelong glance, as if measuring me. "That's because I've never seen a holdup before where someone comes driving up in a buggy. Fellers ride up on horses, take money, watches, jewelry, put it all in the saddlebags. But this gang brought along a damn buggy, pardon my French. I'm thinking they were after you, Shulamit. Or maybe your grandfather's trunk with that go-lem in it. You think?"

Sharp man. Too sharp. I kept my face expressionless and shrugged. I'd had years of experience helping my grandfather keep the golem a secret from my father, my stepmother, and my brothers— I wasn't going to stop now. When my grandfather lay on his deathbed, I'd overheard my family's plans. They'd sell the rebbe's library (his *dreck*, they called it) and rent out his rooms. They'd send me to work in a garment factory. There were already generous offers for my grandfather's old trunk, my father said.

"Can you imagine?" I heard him say. "That heap from the old country?"

"So, ask for more!" my stepmother snapped.

The next morning I contacted a *shadchen* my grandfather had told me about and she quietly set about arranging a new life for me in the New Mexico Territory— a place I imagined to be slightly west of Chicago. Even as we made the plans, fleeing New York with my grandfather's golem seemed fantastic and unlikely— even stranger than becoming a bride, mail-order or otherwise, of a shopkeeper named Morris Saperstein.

But when *Zayde* died, I was ready. Family and neighbors walked from the services at the shul to the cemetery, leaving me to prepare the house for *shivah*. Instead, I called a carter and left with the trunk. Sure enough, the two Kabbalists appeared as we neared the train station. But they'd underestimated the strength of the burly Irish carters I'd hired and my own determination to honor the strange promise I'd made my grandfather. And now, as *Zayde* would have said, here we are.

Billy slapped the reins and the buggy sped up, jolting me back to the present. "Does Saperstein know you have that go-lem creature?"

"Certainly not." My plan was to hide the trunk, telling my husband-to-be that it held bed linens and such. Ideally, it would be forgotten by everyone— including me— and my pact with my grandfather would be honored. Of course, now Billy knew...

"But Saperstein knows you're arriving?"

"Of course he knows," I snapped. "A *shadchen*— a matchmaker— in New York answered his ad on my behalf, and he sent her the money for my travel."

"Beg pardon, Sorry. It's just that I never imagined Morris Saperstein sending off for a mail-order bride."

"And why not?" I bristled. "He wants someone to help with the store, to do the accounts. I did all of that for my grandfather's yeshiva and for my brothers' tailor shop."

Billy shrugged. I reddened and sat silent. I suspected Billy had assessed my looks and thought Saperstein might regret buying goods sight unseen. We rode on in the dark and growing cold of the desert evening. I'd taken my shawl from my carpetbag and now I pulled it tight around me. Outcroppings of rock beside the trail loomed over us. It was all too easy to imagine someone leaping down from those boulders onto the buggy. I shivered.

"Cold?"

"No," I said. "Frightened. Do you think...we should wake the golem?"

"Might not be a bad idea." Billy's voice rang loud in the empty desert. His drawl had grown slower, and he swallowed in a way that made me doubt his courage. He was awfully young.

As I turned on the bench to open the trunk, Billy swore softly. I spun back to see two dark figures ahead on the trail. They wore long black beards and wide black hats, and the little that showed of their faces gleamed pale in the light from the rising moon. Our horse shook its head violently and balked. Billy reached for his gun. "What the—?"

My grandfather's students— or creatures in their form— rose up on columns of dense black smoke, swaying like snakes about to strike.

"The golem! Open the trunk!"

I stammered the words to spring the locks and then grabbed my reticule. *Where was it?* As I rummaged desperately for the twist of paper, tendrils of black smoke embraced me. I smelled tobacco and Russian Caravan tea and wool. The warmth of the coal fire in my grandfather's study in Manhattan. *How lovely!* I closed my eyes and breathed deeply.

"Shulamit!" Billy's shout brought me back to the present. My fingers closed on the twisted paper bearing the Hebrew letters that spelled Truth. I threw back the trunk lid, leaned in and stuffed the paper into the golem's ear.

"Protect me," I mumbled, fighting the hypnotic smoke. "No! Protect *us!*"

The golem awoke, eyes gleaming like rubies. I sank down as it rose up to confront the two dark figures swooping above us, long arms outstretched, hands grasping. One of the figures caught the golem's arms. I lunged for the creature's sturdy legs. I held on tight, anchoring the golem to the buggy, my eyes squeezed shut against the enchanting smoke.

A whip cracked. The buggy jerked into motion. Soon we were tearing down the trail, Billy shouting at the horse, me clutching the golem's legs, the golem battling with dark smoky creatures above us.

An explosion sent us flying into the air. Sand stung my face and wind nearly ripped away my shawl. We landed violently, the buggy tipping on two wheels before settling upright to resume its jolting path down the trail. Billy cursed as he fought to rein in the horse.

I opened my eyes. Great, dark leaves of greasy ash came drifting down through the night. The Kabbalists were gone. The golem had collapsed and sprawled over the side of the trunk.

"Return to the trunk," I ordered as the horse slowed to a ragged trot. To my relief, the golem quickly rearranged itself, settling into the trunk as if exhausted. About to closed the lid, I paused. I placed a trembling hand on its bowed head for a moment. "*A dank*. Thank you."

I extracted the twist of paper from its ear, returned it to my bag, then closed and secured the lid of the trunk. I saw Billy watching me closely. Too closely. *He wants to use the golem for himself*, I realized. *I can't let that happen.*

We drove in silence. A few miles on, we turned off the main trail onto a narrower, winding roadway. Before I could ask where we were going, a low adobe building, its courtyard aglow with lanterns, appeared in a stand of Ponderosa pines. I assumed it was a rustic inn and though how wonderful it would be to bathe and crawl into a real bed.

"I have friends here," was all Billy said. Two grey-haired, dark-skinned women came out to greet us. The elder of the pair showed me to an outbuilding and an adjoining washhouse. The younger one argued with Billy, the two of them speaking a language I thought must be Spanish. When I returned, the older woman had set out food. We tore into it. I'd never tasted chili verde or tortillas before but was too hungry and tired to care if I was eating was *treyf*.

"What we saw out on the road," Billy said to me in a low voice after the woman left the room, "the locals out here would have called them demons or spirits. You knew what they were."

I swallowed a forkful of the spicy stew and coughed, wondering how much I could tell him. "My grandfather taught...what you'd call magic. Those were his students, but bad ones. I'm supposed to be taking the golem where people like them they won't find it."

People like you, either, I thought.

"Magic?" Billy shrugged. "Figured it to be something like that. Those two men looking for you must have hired the boys who held up the stage. Coburn's strongbox would have been their payment for finding your go-lem."

Billy's voice had risen. He lowered it before going on. "Hell, Coburn may have been in on the plan, hiring me so Olinger could have me killed. Those fellows who held us up? I used to ride with them. You're not the only one who has a long story."

So Billy has his own enemies. I wondered why he didn't just move on to another place, but I was too tired to ask. I thought we'd stay the night at the ranch, sleep, and change into clean clothing, but Billy insisted we push on to Lincoln that night. In the ranch house courtyard, our buggy waited with a fresh horse, a solid-looking bay. But grandfather's trunk was gone from the back. I whirled on Billy. "Where is—?"

"Don't ask, Shulamit," he said. "I've put it somewhere safe, and I think we should both forget about it for a time."

"No!" As much as I depended on Billy to get me to Lincoln, I couldn't trust him with the golem. I flew at him, fists raised. He clapped a powerful hand on my shoulder and held me at arms length, shaking his head. In the flickering lantern light, I saw his smile tinged with regret.

"We need to get on into Lincoln tonight," he repeated.

I dropped my fists, turned, and let him hand me up into the buggy.

"You can't use the golem, you know," I warned him as we drove away from the ranch. "You don't know the proper words. And the golem— they say it only works to protect people."

Billy shrugged. "We'll see about that. For the time being, it's safe. And I'm taking you to Kate Flaherty's boardinghouse. You can stay there before you...before you meet Saperstein."

I was sure he'd try to open the trunk and use the golem. On the other hand, I was sure Billy had put it where it would be safe from the two Kabbalists— if they'd survived tonight's battle with the golem, which I hoped they had not.

We swung back onto the trail. The near-full moon rode high over the desert and it lit the way surprisingly well. Coyotes howled. An owl swooped across our path. I didn't trust Billy McCarty, but the cold reality was that he was my only friend in the New Mexico Territory.

"What's he like?" I asked. "Morris Saperstein."

The ad in the New York paper had read: "Handsome, observant Jewish bachelor, 37, doing a good business in dry goods, seeks Jewish maiden or childless widow, 18 to 30, who would like a good home and is willing to assist in the emporium."

"A businessman." Billy adjusted his shoulders in a way that suggested he wasn't telling the whole story.

"Do you think he'll be satisfied with me?" In the darkness, I bit my lip. As my stepmother had missed no occasion to remark, I was no prize: tall as a man, thin as a broomstick, with a sharp nose and a sharp tongue.

"I will be more interested to know if you're satisfied with him," Billy said.

Did I have any choice? The money the *shadchen* had given me for the trip was almost gone. The closer the buggy got to Lincoln the more I wished I'd stayed in New York. We rode on.

"Do you miss New York?" I asked Billy.

A low chuckle. He flicked the reins across the horse's back. "New Mexico Territory suits me just fine."

***

It was well after midnight when we reached Lincoln. It didn't appear to me to be much of a town. Rough adobe buildings lined the main street. Behind them, dirt alleyways gave access to barns, warehouses and stables. We turned into one of those back alleys, Billy stopping the buggy behind a two-story building with lights on downstairs.

Billy slipped up the back steps, light as a cat, stood close to the kitchen door, and knocked softly. When the door opened, he beckoned for me to join him.

"You heard about the holdup?" I heard him say in a low voice as he bundled me into the house.

"Heard there's two of the gang dead and the other one barely got back to town." The woman in the hallway closed the door behind us and threw the lock. "What the hell happened out there? Were you riding with them? Who's this?"

The hallway was dark, but Billy's voice told me that his grin was gone from his face. "I changed sides. Coburn hired me to escort him and his papers to the bank. He's dead."

"What?"

Billy brought me forward. "Shulamit, this is Kate Flaherty. Kate,

173

this is Shulamit Pelz. She's—" Billy hesitated "-- she's a mail-order bride for Saperstein."

"You're having me on." Kate pulled me into kitchen to see me in the lamplight. She was nearly as tall as I was, but there any similarity ended. Kate was a beauty. Her skin was pale and her thick black hair, worn in a bun, was shot through with silver. She had an upturned nose, high cheekbones, and ice-blue eyes. She wore a crisp linen apron over a dove-grey dress. "Billy?"

But he was already down the hall and out the back door.

"Well, would seem that I'm stuck with you, Miss Shula—?" The woman glared.

"Shulamit. Shulamit Pelz."

Shaking her head, Kate picked up a small lamp from a side table and I followed her up the stairs. At the first landing she opened the door to a small room. There was a bed mounded with comforters and pillows. A flowered china basin and a pitcher of water stood on the dressing table. Tears welled in my eyes.

As I walked through the doorway with my bag, she caught my arm. "Someone's going to ask you about what happened out there, Miss Shulamit. Whatever it was, you'll be better off if you forget about it. You just tell them that someone brought you here, unconscious, and I found you on the porch. You don't remember anyone's face, or name."

Kate's grip on my arm tightened. "You never met William McCarty. You never heard of any Billy the Kid. You understand that?"

I dropped the carpetbag and stood with clenched fists. Kate stepped back. She told me later that she was prepared for anything, and was as surprised as I was when I began to cry. Tears filled my eyes again and again, but they didn't wash away images of the day. I made no protest when Kate undressed me, stood me on a towel, and sponged me clean. She tucked my hair into a ruffled cap and dropped a linen gown over my head. She must have led me to the bed as well, because I woke up there in the morning.

Voices were coming from downstairs. I heard Kate's voice and a big booming voice that meant Police. I cracked the door and listened as I dressed, donning a plain cotton blouse Kate had set out and my travel-weary wool skirt.

"Three men out there dead, and it looks like this Miss Pelz is the only witness we have," the man was saying as I came down the stairs.

"What do you think happened, Deputy?" Kate's voice, sweet as honey.

"My guess?" His coffee cup rattled on the saucer. He nodded to me as I entered the parlor. "We know Coburn had hired Billy as a bodyguard. I think Billy double-crossed him, brought in some of his friends. There was more of a shootout than they expected, but Billy made off with the loot."

Now I knew why Kate wanted me to play dumb. When she saw me standing there, she made introductions. She insisted on taking me to the settee and bringing me a cup of fragrant tea and a thick slice of fresh-baked bread.

"What this poor woman has been through!" she said. "Deputy Olinger, do take care with her."

Kate sat close beside me; close enough, I suspected, to be able to give me a quick nudge if my answers strayed in the wrong direction. I did my best convince Olinger that I was a sheltered Jewish spinster. I knew only that I'd been sharing a stagecoach with a businessman and a ranch hand when a terrible holdup had occurred.

"Do you know Billy the Kid?" he asked.

"No, sir, there weren't any children, no," I said, making a show of earnest helpfulness. Kate looked up at the ceiling as if inspecting the chandelier for cobwebs.

The deputy's tanned brow furrowed with puzzlement and frustration. "Did one of the men ask you to open a big trunk?" He spoke slowly, as if to a child, and held his arms wide to indicate the trunk.

I felt Kate stiffen beside me. So the man who rode off with Coburn's strongbox, the survivor, had told someone about my golem. I furrowed back at Olinger. "No, sir. When there were guns, I fainted. Someone brought me here, to Miss Flaherty's boardinghouse, for which I am of course so grateful."

I turned and smiled at Kate, who beamed approvingly at my stilted English. Olinger gave a muffled snort, stood up, clapped his big hat on his head, and muttered a perfunctory thanks.

"Oh, Deputy," I said, brightening. "When will you get my trunk back?"

He glared, assured me they'd do their best to recover the baggage, and left, stomping into the hallway and out the door.

"Nicely played," Kate said. "'There weren't any children,' indeed. We must remember to tell that to Billy."

***

Four years went by. My accounting skills proved the perfect asset for the boardinghouse and the two other properties Kate owned in town. I even took on Morris Saperstein as a client.

For, as it turned out, Morris had never advertised for a mail-order bride. The ad and the money that brought me west were the work of his mother, Etta Saperstein, a formidable widow who lived in an apartment over his dry goods emporium. She'd hoped Morris would marry a nice Jewish girl, but now would have to content herself with a grandchild from Morris' girlfriend Juliette, recently retired from dancing in the Two Pines Saloon.

It took a few months of wrangling, but Kate and I talked Billy into bringing us the trunk. He realized he'd never be able to wake the golem, much less teach it how to ride and shoot.

"Couldn't even open the damned lid," Billy confessed. He delivered the trunk, in the dead of night, to the back porch of the boarding house and the three of us lugged it upstairs. When he left, Kate and I hid it deep in the linen closet.

Billy, of course, could not stay out of trouble. Arrests, escapes, more arrests, and always, the headlines: "Billy the Kid Escapes Again!" Then the Law reneged on its promise to pardon him on a murder charge in return for testimony. He was convicted for the murder and sentenced to hang. Of course, he escaped.

But in April he was re-captured and jailed at the Lincoln County Courthouse. One of our boarders, himself a deputy, related with some distaste how much Deputy Olinger relished making the arrest.

" I knew you'd slip up," Olinger had taunted Billy. "We haven't even taken down the noose. Kept it all ready for you."

Kate and I tried to visit Billy in jail, but Olinger was taking no chances. "You two weird sisters can see 'im when he hangs, just like everyone else."

Kate threw him a withering glare. We walked slowly back to the boardinghouse. She went upstairs to the linen closet while I fetched a small twist of paper that had sat in my desk drawer for nearly four years. We stood for a long while, staring at the dome-top trunk. Kate sighed. "Shulamit, my dear, do your New York magic."

***

That evening, Kate and I watched as Olinger herded the other prisoners across the street to the saloon for their dinner. That left Billy alone in his cell on the jail's second story with a deputy alone in the office downstairs.

I stammered the words, opened the old trunk, and slipped the twist of paper into the golem's ear. Helping him out of the trunk, I brushed some ash, from that night four years ago, from his shoulder. He straightened up, and I thought I saw his small toothless mouth take the shape of a grin. I guided him down the stairs and together we slipped out the back door of the boardinghouse.

"Follow me." I tiptoed down the alley between the bank and the dry goods store, the golem behind me, shuffling barefoot on the hard-packed dirt. Light from the setting sun flooded the alley and threw our shadows on the adobe wall of the bank. The golem loomed two stories high. *A monster.* "Stop here."

We'd reached the mouth of the alley. I looked over at the jail. A sigh of relief: Billy stood at his window, fiddling with the close-set iron bars as if he expected to find a way out. I shook my head. Apparently solutions came to Billy as easily as trouble. *And here we were.*

I whistled. Billy saw me and slowly raised one hand. He watched as I turned and reached up to take the hand of the golem. I pressed the loaded pistol into creature's sun-warmed clay paw.

"Throw this—" I patted the pistol "-- up to that man."

I pointed at Billy. Then I dropped back, leaving the golem to shuffle forward on his own, the gun dangling awkwardly at his side. *Whatever would my zayde have thought?* I wondered as I slipped back down the alley and entered the back door of the boardinghouse. Kate waited for me at the front window. She grabbed my hand, and her slender fingers squeezed. "He's there."

Sure enough, the golem had reached the courthouse. I could see Billy reaching his hand out through the bars. The golem tossed the six-shooter up to Billy just as the deputy emerged from the courthouse door and took a shot at him. The golem shattered into thousands of pieces, leaving the deputy gaping. Above them, Billy had caught the gun and vanished.

The deputy ran back into the jail. Two shots rang out. I gasped with relief as Billy burst from the jail, gun in hand, and ran to the hitching post. Freeing the reins of a small black gelding, he swung up into the saddle. Then he paused.

"Go, go, go," Kate muttered, stamping her boots in a gallop.

But Billy, astride the horse, gun in hand, waited until Olinger burst from the saloon across the street. Then Billy took aim and fired two shots. Olinger toppled face down in the street.

Billy the Kid turned the horse, spurred it, and galloped away into the purple twilight.

By then men were pouring into the street, calling for horses and guns and the town doctor. A posse formed in front of the courthouse, trampling the shards that had once been a golem before whirling and clattering north after Billy.

Soon darkness fell on the empty street. The wind swept in from the desert. Kate went upstairs after a while and I heard the lid snap shut on a hollow, empty trunk. She came down again, and led me gently from the window. But not before I'd watched a twist of white paper go swirling off into the night.

Thank You To Our Supporters

Many thanks to our patrons and supporters, especially:

Anna O'Brien • Cathrin Hagey • S Naomi Scott
Natalie Weizenbaum • Siobhan Beeman

Emily Anderson • Felicia OSullivan • Fen
J'nae Spano • Martin Cohen • Salomao Becker
Shelly Jones • Tessa N • Tory Hoke

S. Kay Nash • Carly Racklin • GriffinFire
Isabel Cañas • Jen G • Kayla • Liz Warner
Maria Haskins • Suzanne Thackston

Want to see your name here? Become a patron!
patreon.com/lunastation

About the Cover Artist

Shreya Shetty is a concept artist/illustrator based in Los Angeles. She worked in-house at Rhythm and Hues Studios as a texture painter and a concept artist on a variety of movies and pitch projects. She freelances for various clients and her personal work focuses on fantasy themes, particularly mythology, culture and creatures.

You can find more of her work at:

shreyashetty.com

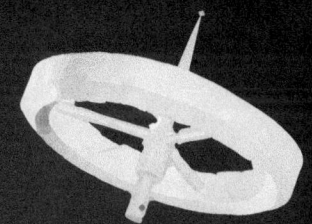

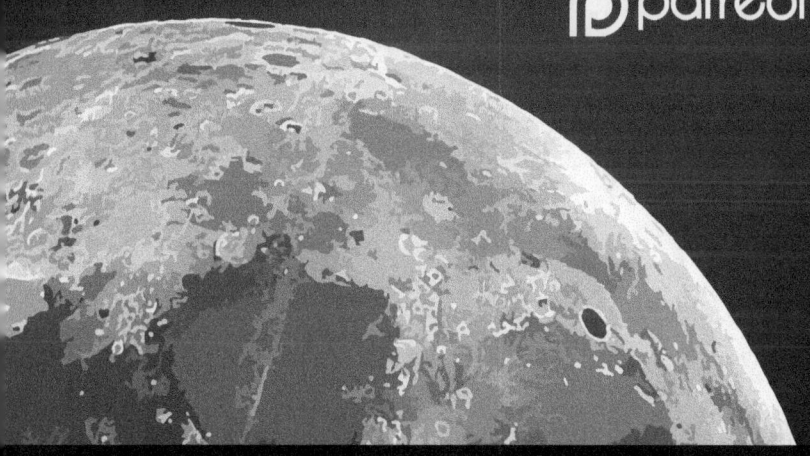